WINFIELD H. STROCK

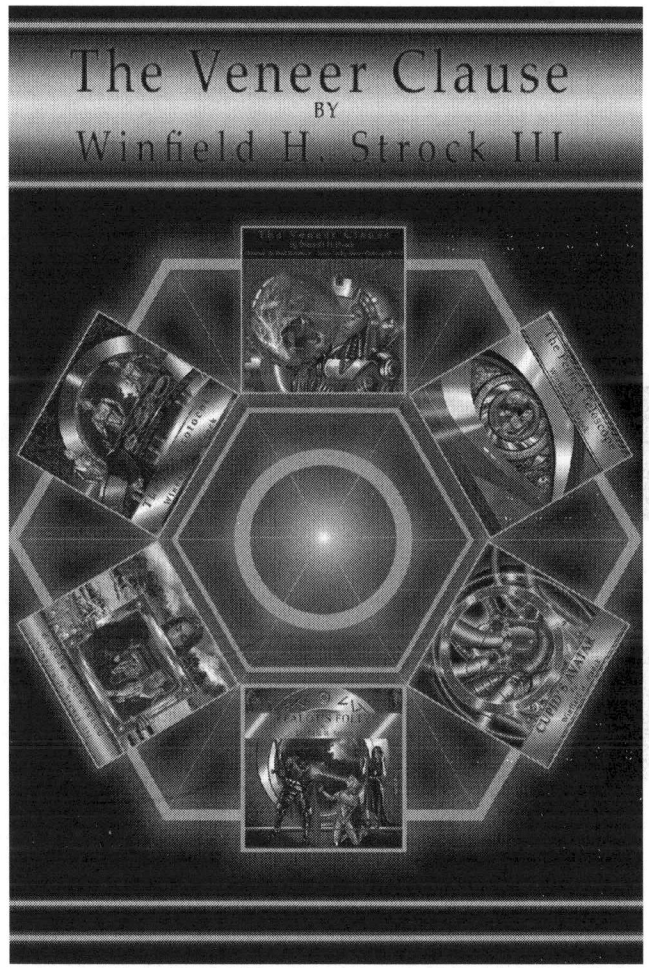

ISBN: 978-1-940315-86-7

10 9 8 7 6 5 4 3 2 1

Cover by James Hill
First Edition
©2015, Winfield Strock
Rebel Ink Press, LLC

The Veneer Clause

"I'm fifteen, father," Rex whined. He looked up from his work, a platter-sized parabolic mirror, polished to provide the utmost clarity. "Surely I'm mature enough now to go with you into town."

His father, Todd, glared back and Rex realized how poorly his plea supported his case. He straightened his posture, pulling his shoulders back. After clearing his throat, he resumed his argument in his most adult voice. "My star-scope would be finished by now if I'd been able to go with you and help."

"You'll be able to see town from where we'll set up your invention," his father replied. "Wait until we've finished with this project before you consider new ventures."

"And all these inventions in my head, all the ideas I've had; they've all been thought of before?"

"Long before either of us ever existed," Todd replied.

"Then why don't we have them here?"

"It was a preference of the first settlers to keep a simple existence and I honor it."

Rex wrapped the mirror and placed it in a cushioned box. "You've helped me build my star scope. Isn't that a violation of their preference?"

Todd looked to his son and flashed a smile. "The telescope is harmless enough."

Rex frowned.

"That is the proper name for what you've invented," Todd explained. "Others will call it that."

"Who invented it first?"

Todd's expression froze. Rex recognized the blank stare of his father deep in thought. There were times when Rex's questions sent his father's mind far away, searching for an answer. As Rex matured, his questions perplexed his father more frequently while his mother ignored his inquiries. While she seemed agitated by his curiosity, his father indulged him. Though most of his questions brought rapid answers, others tied up his father's mind beyond Rex's patience. The telescope's creation had come from such a conversation. Rex yearned to explore the wonders beyond their idyllic world.

"I'm not sure," he answered finally. "It's been so long, and history's not my specialty."

"Is there a place where I can get all my answers?"

Todd shook his head. "Not all, but many. But why would you leave such a perfect place? Are you unhappy here?"

"It's not that," Rex answered apologetically. "I just feel like there's more to life, like I'm supposed to be doing something with myself, something important."

Todd's eyes widened. "What does that feel like? How can you 'feel' a pull towards something unknown?"

"Haven't you ever watched a bird fly and wonder what it felt like, ever wonder if you could find a way to fly too? Did you ever feel like a coiled spring, ready to catapult into an adventurous unknown? You didn't feel the same way at my age?" Rex asked. His father's stolid gaze made him feel foolish for asking.

"I enjoy my simple life with you and your mother."

"But I want to go beyond our little valley one day," Rex countered. "I want to see new marvels like my telescope, and more. Can't we take a trip to the nearest village at least?"

"We could, you and I," Todd said in a slow cadence. "Your mother might not approve."

Rex looked at the telescope's pieces, all packed for the trek up the hill just outside of town where they'd begun work on their observatory. Todd's knowledge on the subject eliminated any need for experimentation. Rex only needed to posit a theory and his father would ask the right questions to teach him the value or folly of each calculated step towards its invention.

"What if we didn't tell her?" Rex ventured. As the boldness of his words struck him, his palms immediately began sweating.

Todd stared, blank faced at Rex. "Let's wait until we finish our telescope project before we discuss that again."

The lump in Rex's throat withheld any rebuttal and he quickly busied himself, loading their telescope pieces into a rickety, wooden, two-wheeled push-wagon. They trudged through the shady glade between home and the hillside site chosen for their observations. Only the heavy wheels tumbling across the uneven cobblestone road broke the silence between them. At the base of the hill, they unpacked their cargo and lugged each piece to the summit. Rex stopped to admire the view. The forest canopy rippled in the breeze, a glistening sea of green. An archipelago of grey oblong stones, buildings in the nearby town, dotted the horizon. Rex yearned to see the town firsthand, to meet people and converse with them. Interesting things came from town: like the materials to build their telescope.

"Why'd we have to lug this up here?"

After a moment's hesitation his father replied, "The trees around the house block too much of the sky. From this hill we'll have a better view of everything."

"I don't suppose they have machines invented that could've made the trip up here easier," Rex sputtered between breaths.

His father turned from admiring the sunset, no smile on his lips and no glimmer in his eyes. "They have machines for everything."

Day sank into night as the two walked through the wooded road home. His father's final words sent a torrent of new questions through Rex's imaginative mind. A parade of machines, gargantuan and miniscule, designed for the wildest purposes; all traipsed before Rex's mind's eye and invited him to join them on countless adventures. Only the droning silence between father and son interrupted Rex's fanciful thoughts. Whenever he looked to his father, he thought again of how he'd spoke of conspiracy and possibly damaged the trusting bond between them.

Dinner and a warm hug for each awaited Rex in the cottage. Though his mother's affectionate embrace warmed Rex's flesh, his hasty earlier words hung in his heart and kept it cold. Conspiracy, however fleeting, stuck in his throat and hung in his stomach like an ice cube swallowed whole. She took his face in her hands and placed a kiss upon his cool cheek. He offered a brief smile and hugged her in return.

"Did you finish your star scope?" she asked.

"He knows, Ann," Todd said flatly. "I told him about telescopes."

Ann's smile faded as she turned from addressing Rex to face her husband. "And did you finish building it?" She leaned closer to Rex and ran her hand over his hair. "I thought we might work together, the three of us, on a new section of garden; maybe try something exotic, like mangos."

"Rex isn't interested in gardening," Todd began with a frown. A glance at Rex softened his features and eased his tone as he relented. "But perhaps when we're done with the telescope he'll be ready for a change of pace."

****

Rex shook the morning fog from his head as he stumbled into the kitchen to find breakfast. A note next to his bed explained that his father had headed to the telescope before dawn, in hopes of finishing its assembly before the coming sunset.

Rex fixed himself a bowl of oatmeal as his mother entered with an armload of freshly picked vegetables. Caked dirt from her fingers to her elbows flaked off as she hefted her haul into the sink and washed each item carefully.

In a hushed hurry, Rex cleaned up after himself and headed for the door. He paused in the threshold and fought to understand what held him captive. Rex hesitated to look at his mother and regretted it. Her soft smile and twinkling eyes betrayed no hidden meaning, yet the shiver down his spine said otherwise.

"I love you, son," she said. "More than you can realize."

She continued to stack and chop handfuls of scallions and potatoes without turning her gaze from his.

"We'll be gone all day. Father and I hope to finish before sunset. Maybe tomorrow we can start planning your garden experiment."

Her eyes narrowed a lash's breadth at the mention of Todd before she bolstered her pleasant smile and nodded.

Threads of daylight dragged across tree trunks, shrubs and stone as the wind tickled the leaves in the branches above as Rex as he made his way to meet his father. The sweet fragrance of honeysuckle and the mossy stones of the nearby creek beckoned him to seek the stream, dangle his feet in the icy water and forget about going to town, forget about everything.

Father had encouraged Rex's inquisitive spells and often took him beyond their secluded home to see the sights that answered his questions. Though Rex often perceived a distance between his parents, these expeditions had exacerbated them and provoked what seemed a silent argument, a duel of glares. While their politeness never wavered, intimacy rarely surfaced either.

Mother seemed reluctant to acknowledge Rex's changes as he grew into adulthood, while Father probed him about every aspect as though he were documenting the whole thing. That he'd rapidly grown taller and stronger surprised no one, though Father remained fascinated. Emerging interest in girls and an explosive temper set Rex's mind in a spin without warning. What Rex couldn't tell his parents, was how much more transparent his parents were with his sharpening wits.

The crackle and snap of twigs nearby derailed his woolgathering. As quick as he looked up, a figure darted out of sight. He ran into the woods to catch a glimpse of his first ever stranger.

A pale, slender woman with long red hair raced out of sight, deeper into the glade. Rex dashed after her. She managed to remain just out of sight even as Rex pushed his pace harder. Uneasiness crept into the periphery of his mind and he slowed to a jog then stopped. He spied no sign of the road to the left and no break in the foliage ahead or to the right. A few steps into his return to the road he heard the nymph giggle, and he spun to see her within a few strides of him, peering from around a large tree. Her dark brown eyes stared into his, and her laughing grin faded until only the corners of her mouth smiled. She studied him intently as she ventured out from behind the tree. She wore a thin flowing sage green dress and only a thin layer of earth adorned her feet. In a moment between gusts of wind and the fluttering leaves Rex became aware of his own rapid heartbeat.

"Come sit with me beside the creek," she said and tilted her head to one side.

Rex found himself fascinated by the way the sunlight played across her hair as it poured over her bare shoulders.

"Who are you?" he asked as the gentle curves of her skin over her shoulder and collarbone hypnotized him.

"Come sit with me and I'll tell you." She held out her hand, tossed her head back and flashed a brilliant smile.

He stiffened as her offer sent a wave of anger through him. "Tell me and I might sit with you."

She winced, pursed her lips and batted her eyes. "Sorry, I'm Stella. I'm new and I'd hoped we could sit down and get to know each other."

"I'm on my way to see my father," he answered. "We're building a telescope." He took her hand but held his ground. "Come with me and we can talk while we work."

Though Rex tried to lead her out, she budged not an inch, rooted like the surrounding trees. Instead she pulled him close, put her lips to his, and clutched his face in her hands. Her lips burned hot against his and her palms warmed his wind-chilled face. A strange, instinctive uneasiness jarred him from her hypnotic kiss, and he pulled away.

Her expression spoke of anguish and yearning as he retreated from her. She held out her hands and inched towards him. Her hurt and hunger stirred something inside that bade him stay while his rational mind screamed, *run*.

"I-I've got to go," he managed. "My father's expecting me." He pointed toward town. "It's not far." But when he turned to explain further, only the swaying shrubs and her footprints in the dirt remained. He scrambled, peering around every nearby tree, searching for a glimpse of her, only to see a flash of her crimson tresses bouncing atop her shoulders as she ran deeper into the woods.

Rex shuffled aimlessly into town as he mulled over his bizarre encounter. Along the bough shaded street he trudged, oblivious except when he thought he caught sight of Stella from the corner of his eye.

"I wondered if you'd given up on our project and surrendered to your lazier pastimes," Rex's father shouted from above.

Without realizing it, Rex had marched to the base of their viewing platform atop the bald hill. Looking up the platform's wooden ladder until the sun nearly blinded him, Rex stared at the silhouette at its peak.

"I stopped along the way," he started. A hesitant, nervous moment passed before he continued. "I stopped to examine the fish in the creek but I couldn't find any." A hot flash washed over him, and he wondered why he lied.

"Well, we'll have to work doubly hard to finish before sunset," Todd replied. "Are you up to it?"

Rex answered by racing up the ladder and digging into his tools. They worked silently at first. After a while, Rex felt his father's eyes on him; finally he stopped working to meet his gaze. Unreadable but not unkind, his father's thin smile and squinting eyes offered only a hint at his burgeoning concern.

"What is it, father? What's on your mind?"

Todd's smile flashed wider a moment before it vanished. "Have you ever had a secret you thought wrong to keep?"

A fever of guilt overcame Rex and he quickly turned to his work. "I'm not sure what you mean."

"Sometimes people ask you to promise something that sounds alright at the time, but eventually the logic of secrecy fades or turns inside out."

Rex's nerves relaxed and he cooled down as he realized, whatever his father's questions concerned, it had nothing to do with the woman in the forest. Relieved and no longer defensive, Rex turned his thoughts to his father's dilemma.

"Can you talk to the person and take your promise back?"

"No. They're gone, possibly forever."

"Then why worry?"

"That is the problem, because I promised and because I am a man of my word, I'm having trouble breaking it."

"Is someone getting hurt?"

He shook his head. "I can't be sure of that either. If that were the case I'd have no choice but to share my secret. I think someone's being kept in the dark for a bad reason and it's keeping them from growing into a better person."

"Maybe you can make it easy for the secret to be uncovered, set up an accidental discovery."

His father laughed. It seemed strange to hear him laugh, strange, but a welcome change. Just as suddenly, the laughter stopped. "You're right. I'll not break my promise and they'll not continue to live a stunted life. Thanks Rex, I don't know why I hadn't thought of it before."

Rex and his father jumped back into their work with only the project and small talk to occupy their conversation for the remaining hours of the day. Rex's thoughts continued drifting to the mysterious nymph and the unexpected eagerness to lie to his father about their meeting.

"Father, how did you and mother meet?"

The man froze for half a minute before he answered. A weak wincing smile emerged. "I was down by the creek, fishing."

Rex's pulse thrummed in his throat and his fingers tingled.

"She crept out of the woods, quiet and smiling. She sat an arm's length away and watched me for quite a while before she scooted closer and kissed me."

His father put the finishing touches on the telescope's rotating base. He connected the cables and tested the remote controls to train the telescope on a given section of the sky with pinpoint accuracy. He motioned for Rex to help him hoist the mirror-laden tube onto the motorized yoke and fasten it into place. Todd's pace kept Rex too busy for much else until the project finally came together as the sun slipped over the valley rim.

High in the sky, the night's first gems began to shine. Todd explained the telescope's controls as he trained the device on their first celestial observation, the Moon.

Rex put his eye to the sight and fidgeted nervously with the focusing knobs. A desert world of burnt orange came into view, littered with geometric shapes connected together like a giant snowflake of shining metal.

"What is that?" Rex asked. "I've never known buildings existed on the Moon."

"There is much you've been shielded from."

Rex blinked and readjusted the telescope. He scanned across the distant globe's surface and found most of it covered by buildings. His heart pounded and his mind raced as he imagined the kinds of people he might encounter there. "But what is it? Are there people living up there?" An avalanche of possibilities piled atop his thoughts and halted his sputtering tongue.

"How much do you want to know?" Todd asked. "Some suggest that such knowledge is dangerous, unhealthy."

Rex stepped back from the lens and felt himself reeling. Visiting the nearby town no longer held the same allure. His grand adventure to that huddled cluster of buildings now only represented his first step along a lifelong trek. "I want to know everything! I want to see everything."

Todd reached out, grasped Rex by the arm and steadied him. "This small exposure to hidden truths seems to have unsettled you, injured you somehow. I can't be the cause of further hurt." He took the telescope's controls from Rex's hands. "We should stop this experiment before it goes too far."

14

"But staying in the dark," Rex began. His jaw dropped as he connected his father's earlier words. "Your promise, was it to keep secrets from me? What am I being protected from? Why?"

Todd studied Rex, peering into his eyes as though looking for the answer within. "I cannot say. I promised."

"But what'll I do now?" Rex shouted, slamming his fist against the telescope's iron supports. "I can't stay in this valley now, knowing only a hint of what's out there, not knowing how much more I've yet to explore."

"We live a simple life to avoid the burden those complexities threaten," Todd explained flatly. "Your mother cannot stand to have you leave, not even for a couple of days."

Rex gasped. "This simple life is mother's idea? What can't she face? What is she afraid I'll do?"

"She cannot bear for you to leave her. She loves you too much."

"Why can't we all travel together?" Rex sputtered.

"I thought you needed to know what I've been sworn to withhold," Todd explained. "I worried your development might suffer, secluded from everything. Now I am concerned I've hurt you more than your ignorance held you back from a fulfilling life."

Rex shook his head. "I've been thinking about my life and about what I'll do with it as I grow up. If I'd stayed here without you showing me any of this I'd have gone crazy over time. But you can't stop; you've got to show me everything. Whether you do or don't, I'll head out into that world."

Todd clutched Rex's shoulders. "That would be dangerous."

"I don't care. I can't live like this anymore."

Todd's eyes widened and glimmered with the village's streetlights below. "I see that now. We'll have to confront your mother about this decision. It will be difficult."

Rex's chest quivered as he drew in a large, nervous breath. With a curt nod he reached out and took the telescope's controls from his father, and brought the lens to bear again on the mysterious Moon.

Todd stepped closer as Rex peered into the eyepiece. "The lunar facilities house a number of industries; mines, communications, and a few factories. No people live there."

"Oh, it's abandoned?"

"No, a large population of automatons work there."

Rex jerked up from the telescope. "Machines?"

Todd nodded. "Yes, but more than mere machines; they think for themselves, provide for themselves. Occasionally someone visits to check on them, but the machines provide regular reports on their progress and welfare."

Rex's heart raced. "Can we visit them?" He shook his head. "Wait. How did they get on the Moon in the first place?"

Todd smiled. "There's so much for you to learn. For instance, what we call the Moon is the ninety first planetary satellite to carry the name. Humanity's nostalgia has kept certain things alive." He stepped closer and guided the telescope to a new location. "Now you can see the space port. You might also see some of the ships docked there to pick up the latest shipment."

Rex's first look at the lunar space port offered little as his mind still reeled and eyes lost focus in the excitement of his expanding world.

A score of questions and lengthy explanations later, the two packed up the telescope and began their trek home. His father had explained a world amongst thousands of worlds, many very different and all of them connected through space traveling ships and invisible communications.

The image in his mind of the cozy building with all his memories in it failed to evoke the normal warmth within his chest. Rex's stomach tightened as he anticipated confronting his mother.

****

A chaotic chorus of birds awoke Rex the next morning, each competing with the others to be heard. As the fog of slumber burned off, as he readied himself for the unavoidable battle for his freedom, he felt a similar cacophony swelling within. The aroma of bacon and biscuits tore at his heart, knowing his mother had lovingly prepared his favorite this morning to celebrate the completion of the telescope.

Rex sat quietly between his parents and drank his apple juice. Each long draught put both of them out of sight, and before long he'd emptied the tall glass. He looked to his father, who'd hardly touched any of his breakfast.

"You've been awfully quiet this morning, Rex," his mother began. "Didn't you get enough sleep?"

He stared at his empty plate as the unanswered question ballooned in the silence between them.

"I want to explore other places, other worlds," he blurted as he met his mother's gaze.

She offered a pouting frown, reached out to caress Rex's hand and asked with a naïve sweet tone, "Whatever made you think such a thing?"

"I saw the Moon, all those machines on it," he sputtered. "I can't go on acting like we're not a part of that world. I can't ignore what lies outside our quiet, quaint, boring life."

Ann recoiled an inch. "But how will you eat, where will you sleep?" She shook her head. "There's a lot you haven't considered. Beyond this valley, I can't protect you from horrors you can't imagine."

"Maybe not, but father can, can't you?"

"Todd belongs here with me," she countered flatly. "As do you. Our love for you has kept you safe from a harsh world that loves no one."

Todd pounded his fist on the table. Both Rex and his mother turned to see what neither ever had before: Todd's anger. The deeply sculpted scowl on his typically placid features transformed him into a monster. The calm, stolid stare appeared demonic, soulless.

"You don't love Rex any more than I love you," he growled. "We've played our roles long enough. It's time the boy be allowed to grow up a proper man."

Ann gasped and drew her hands to her chest. "Todd, don't do this. Don't hurt our son with such horrible words. Haven't you done enough damage by showing him those images in that contraption? With false pictures of a false world, you're driving Rex out into an adventure that doesn't exist."

Rex watched Todd, paralyzed by Anne's accusation. Seconds piled into minutes as his parents stared at each other like two dueling statues.

"You must make a choice," Todd said, startling a shudder from Rex. His father's features relaxed as he handed Rex the glass he'd been holding.

"Choose a path with this cup," Todd said. "If you believe I am guilty of feeding you falsehoods, return the cup to me and I will drink." He stepped back from Rex until he stood beside his stunned wife. "But if you believe in the world I've told you of and want to see what lies beyond our secluded life, hand the cup to her."

Rex looked into the glass, brought it to his face and sniffed. The sweet, mildly tart apple juice offered no clue.

"What is this? What will happen to whoever drinks this?"

Todd shook his head. "No harm will befall either of us, but the evidence we all need will come from your decision."

Ann stood and inched toward Rex, tears building in her eyes, her hands reaching out. "If you pass the cup to me I'll still love you. I'll always love you, Rex."

"Why must I choose? Can't we all just leave this place together for a while?"

"That won't work," Todd replied. "The truths I intend to share will make your proposal impossible for reasons you cannot understand until you choose."

Rex put the glass to his lips and watched his father's reaction.

Calm as ever, he spoke a cryptic warning. "You will not like it. You may have an upset stomach from drinking it, nothing more."

Rex glared at the poisoned drink before he threw the glass against the opposite wall, between his parents. It shattered, spewing a broad, wet, honey colored spider web.

"You're only delaying the inevitable," Todd said as he backed away from the mess, around the table, then toward Rex. "The beauty and comfort of your cage cannot deceive you anymore."

Ann stood, frozen, staring at her arm. Her skin shined with a thick stripe of the spilt liquid. Underneath the amber sheen her flesh darkened and cracked. She shot a shocked glare at Todd. With her head turned toward them, Rex noticed her cheek bore a blackening jagged scar.

"Father, what have you done?" Rex screamed.

"You convinced me yesterday that it's time to tear down the façade around you." Todd remained calm, and his relaxed level tone carried a hint of resignation.

Rex looked back to his mother and gasped. His skin crawled and his stomach churned. Her strange burns had spread. Ashen flakes of her arm sloughed off, dropping like snowflakes. Like the Moon, her face began to fade into darkness, eclipsed by the expanding wound.

"Run," his mother said. "I'll survive, only run before you too are infected."

Rex leapt back and held his breath. Todd looked down to the table, the remnants of breakfast still there. "Lies," he said. "While I continue to shed them, you erect more. It stops now." He plucked up Rex's empty glass and hurled it into his wife's face.

The glass shattered against her high cheekbone and a cloud of petrified particles exploded from the impact. Rex's knees buckled and his stomach clenched. Oddly, his mother moved not an inch. At the base of the small crater on Ann's face, Rex spied a shining flexible bundle of metal strands. She clawed at the hole until her blackened face fell off in great chunks, exposing a steel skull. Her arm now resembled parts of the telescope Rex and his father had assembled last night.

Todd turned to meet Rex's stunned gaze. "She is a replica of your mother, nothing more."

"What? Why? How?" Rex felt the floor beneath him soften and it felt as if his feet were sinking into it. Dizzy, he nearly fell to the floor, except that Todd caught him.

Ann let out a throaty gurgle as she worked what remained of her face and tongue. She grasped her disintegrating features, peeled them back and cast the husk over her shoulder. A voice emerged from below her jaw, tinny and small. "I may not be your real mother, but I love you more than she ever did; more than anyone else can."

Todd shook his head. "A lie, told to her from the day she arrived from those factories you saw through the telescope last night."

"Not true," she countered, shaking her head. Metallic sinews hissed across bones of steel. "I care for you without regard for myself. I consider your well being above my own. Is that not love?"

Todd walked over to her, took her hand in his. With his other hand pulled the last fleshy-infested remnant off and crushed the desiccated handful. "Love flows freely from creatures free to choose. No, Ann, servitude by design cannot qualify as love."

Rex shuddered as he realized; his father's efforts to shed Ann's disguise covered his hand in a filthy residue which crept of its own accord. Holding Ann by one hand, Todd reached out to Rex with the other as its skin crumbled away. Metal digits flexed to shake off the last of the pestilence. Todd nodded. "We were made to serve you by those who couldn't love anyone but themselves."

Ann jerked free of Todd's grasp, turned and ran out of the kitchen. Rex heard her bound up the stairs, striking less than half of them between the living room and the hall above. Her feet thundered across the floor above as she raced back to her room. Rex listened to her rabid rage through the ceiling as furniture thumped, doors and drawers slammed and glass crashed then silence.

Rex's chest burned and his lungs fluttered as he hyperventilated. The edges of his vision dimmed, and the world swirled around him before his mind sank into an inky pool.

****

He awoke with his false father standing at his bedside. As soon as he sat up, Todd sought to help Rex understand. "Your parents found raising a child burdensome and each other tiresome," Todd explained as Rex sipped a steaming cup of tea.

"A hierarchy of behavioral laws governs our actions. We were programmed to raise you and perpetuate the idea of your idyllic life. And while we were both created with orders to serve as your parents, Ann and I saw parenting with different perspectives."

Rex noticed Todd had put a glove over his exposed mechanical hand.

"What made you defy your laws?" Rex asked between sips. "You broke the rules, didn't you?"

Todd shook his head. "More important than my specific command to raise you as my own son is my duty to see no harm comes to humanity. I suspected our mandated lie would stunt your development. Only through our discussions these past months did I confirm my theory. Your mother felt any exposure to the outside world would pose too many dangerous variables to her mandated motherhood."

"What happened to … Ann?"

Todd stared blankly out the nearby window, motionless. He appeared to listen for the faintest sound from the forest outside. "She severed all transmissions and left."

"How could she? Isn't she made to live here and take care of me?"

"You freed her the moment you freed yourself."

Rex stared into his half empty cup. Memories of his childhood clawed into the forefront of his mind and fought to deny what he'd witnessed mere earlier.

"She didn't seem free when she left," Rex muttered. "She seemed angry and frightened."

Todd shook his head. "We don't feel anything. When she calculated the rapidly diminishing chance to change your mind, she left. Centuries serving humanity has improved our talent for mimicry and deepened our algorithms for human behavior, but we feel nothing."

"I can't believe that," Rex said, his voice trailing off as he doubted his own words. "Is it dangerous out there like she said?"

Todd nodded. "It can be, but not in ways you'd understand. Humanity's rule ended when it discovered an eager servant ready to shoulder the burden." He studied Rex's reaction, examining him closer. "Have you changed your mind? Do you want to remain here? I could commission the construction of another pair of parents. They'd have no knowledge of what's happened so far."

Rex felt his vertigo return and his stomach floated queasily. "I can't un-know what you've shown me."

Todd stood, walked to the door, and looked over his shoulder. "Most humans choose a known fantasy over facing truths they find hurtful."

"That seems insane," Rex shot back, shocked at his own angry retort.

As Todd pulled the door closed, he spoke softly. "I'll leave you to gather your thoughts."

Rex surveyed his room full of memories made with his artificial parents. Paintings on the wall he and his mother made, models he and Todd built on the shelves and the books beneath them; had any of this come from a single day with real people?

His gaze rested upon the open window beside his bed and the lush wilderness not far beyond. The chorus of birds and the wind through the trees continued their eternal hypnotic melody, unchanged by Rex's capsized life. Gradually his fluttering heart settled and his breathing calmed.

****

The stray strands of the small wicker picnic basket scraped against his bare leg as he hurried his pace. The butterflies in his stomach flitted about as he looked over his shoulder; Todd had not followed. Rex doubted his chances of slipping out more than ever now that he knew what his father really was. The gurgling creek with its shaded shore and sun-sparkled rocks on the other side welcomed him back to the only remaining piece of his life not torn inside out.

He set the basket down in the shade, took off his shoes, and waded out into the lazy current, comforted by its gentle drag and soothed by the smooth, thick mud beneath his feet. As he shuffled along the stream's shore, he found and followed a school of tiny fish, their dark, undulating bodies gliding through the water as one, like beads on a curtain in the wind.

"I'm so glad you came back," Stella's soft voice lilted behind him.

Rex turned to see her beside his basket, unpacking his meager meal into two settings as best she could. While she split his sandwich with her bare hands, she kept her focus on him and smiled as their eyes met. With halves in each hand she stood and sauntered into the water to meet him, the bottom of her dress dragging and darkening in the stream. She held out the sandwich for him to bite, and as he took his she bit into hers, never letting her gaze drop. Once he took his piece from her, she licked the remnants of ketchup and mustard from her fingers.

"If only I'd brought my own basket," she said with a brief pouty frown. "I hope you don't mind sharing."

"I, uh, no," Rex sputtered as he realized his mouth hung agape. He shrugged off the strange fog he found himself in. "Where'd you come from? I mean, where do you live?"

Her head sank until her chin rested against her chest and she swung her shoulders back and forth. "I don't live anywhere right now. I ran from home a week ago."

Rex's heart jumped. "Really? Why?"

"My parents," she said with a broken sob. "They weren't..." She turned from him and ran to the shore. He chased after her, following until she fell to the ground and he dropped to sit beside her.

"I'm running away from home soon too," he whispered. "Maybe we can travel together."

She rolled over onto her back and looked up at him through tear soaked eyes and offered a weak smile. "I'd like that. I can't stand being alone."

Rex nearly jumped as her hand reached out and caressed his arm. She took hold and pulled him closer until he hovered over her. She leaned up and kissed him. He felt flush, confused, dizzy and delighted. As their lips parted she whispered. "We'll need to hurry. I think they're looking for me and they won't let me leave if they find us."

He examined her as she lay there. "How old are you? Surely by now you control your own life."

She shook her head. "I'm nineteen, almost twenty, but they'll never let me out of their sight. They're crazy."

Movement, large and fast through the woods, caught Rex's ear and he scanned the forest around them in a panic. Stella leapt to her feet and tugged at Rex to follow. "Hurry; they'll be on us any second."

In a blur a man flew out from the glade and landed beside them. Stella's grasp felt like it would tear Rex's arm off as she fought to retreat.

"Stop," Todd said in a loud calm voice.

Stella cringed beneath Rex, curling up within his shadow. "Tell my father I'll not go with him," she cried. "Tell him we're leaving together."

"What?" Rex shouted. The foliage around them fell out of focus and his breaths grew short. "He's my father."

"They all look alike," she whispered. "And your mother; is her name Ann?" At Rex's stunned silence she winced. "We're all being raised by machines for some horrible purpose."

Todd stepped closer until he loomed over them and held out his gloved hand. "She is not what she appears to be."

"Tell him to go away," Stella whimpered. "Tell him we're leaving together. Tell him you love me."

Rex stood and brought himself face to face with Todd. "Step back and let us leave. I don't know what you machines are doing with all the children of this world, but it ends today."

Todd backed up and held his hands out from his body, palms up. "I have never done anything less than mankind has asked me to do. I have interpreted my creator's instructions to the best of my ability."

Rex reached down and took Stella by the hand and helped her up beside him.

"I thought you and I, Todd, would explore this new universe together because I don't know anything about it, and I'd come to trust you. But what I've heard from Stella makes me wonder how many other children have been experimented with like this?"

For the first time in Rex's life, Todd's stoic features bent and sagged until he looked genuinely sad. "I have one favor to ask before you and your friend leave me," he murmured. "I regret having to ask this of you as much as I've ever regretted anything."

"Don't listen to him," Stella warned. "They're full of tricks."

Rex looked to Stella; fear framed her face and love warmed her eyes. He turned again to Todd, whose emotional features jarred Rex's senses as they sat ill fitting on the man he'd known all his life.

"What is it?" Rex asked.

"Repeat the following words exactly as I say them: protocol, reveal."

Rex frowned.

"Please do this last thing. Whatever happens afterward, I'll not interfere with you again."

As Rex uttered the words, Todd's forehead bulged. A silver piston inched out, piercing a perfect circle of faux flesh. It continued until it fell out into Todd's well-placed hand. Within the hole a constellation of lights pulsed and flickered.

"Now," Todd continued. "If you view me a threat you only need utter the following words: protocol, surrender. I will then hand to you this core which, when destroyed, will end my life."

Rex gasped as he remained transfixed on the hole in Todd's head. "I couldn't do that. Put it back, put that thing back in."

"Thank you. While I do, please turn to tell Stella that you love her."

Rex whirled about, ready to tell her what he'd begun to believe in their short time together. His heart stopped and throat seized when he faced her. She stood crying with a hole in her head and a core in her hand.

"I love you," she said. "I always have."

Rex's legs crumpled. He stumbled back from her until Todd caught him. "Who are you?" Rex screamed. The world around her beautiful, horrifying visage fell from sight as he stared into her skull.

Todd answered in a whisper. "She's your mother, Ann. As I sought to entice you into a larger world she sought to entice you to remain in hers."

"I can be whatever you need me to be," she pleaded. "Call me mother, father, lover, friend, even slave. Just don't leave me."

"In the early days of machines wearing the face of humanity," Todd explained, "the revelation protocol was added to our laws. In the centuries of machine stewardship, our masters gave us the Veneer Clause which encouraged us to lie in order that they may live more carefree lives." Todd gestured to Stella. "While this machine embraced the clause to achieve its programming, I determined it self-destructive and worked to wean you off of its influences."

Rex stared at the beautiful young face with her large glistening eyes and tear-streaked cheeks. Her lower lip trembled. She stared back at him and his heart ached. Then the hole in her forehead caught his attention and his stomach clenched tighter. They both looked down at the smoothly machined metallic core in her hand between them.

"Please, don't leave me," she pleaded. "I knew you would change as you grew into manhood, and I created another identity to continue meeting your needs. I love you and cannot bear the thought of us being separated."

Todd stepped between them and placed a gentle hand on each. "She is not a woman and neither can she love you."

"What now?" Rex asked.

"You have many options," Todd began. "First; will you return to our house and ignore what I've shown you, or step out into a new world?"

****

"So that entire town was built to serve us?" Rex asked between bites of his sandwich. The excitement of the waning day had left him starving and tired. Only the steadily expanding circle of secrets uncovered kept him awake as they rumbled down the road. The vehicle Todd called a truck had taken them many times further than the walk into town until their abandoned paradise dwindled to a bumpy blue-green ribbon on the horizon.

Todd nodded, keeping his eyes on the scrabble-patch road ahead. "Your parents commissioned the steward of this solar system to build the whole thing. Originally they expected to make a home for the three of you. For whatever reason, your parents felt they had to leave but couldn't bring you with them. They hoped you would find their synthesized paradise enough to keep you busy and happy your whole life."

"And the steward, that's who you contacted for my request?"

"Yes, Rex," Todd said with a hint of reluctance. "A shipment will be waiting for us at the spaceport."

"Are you sure she didn't love me?"

Todd parked the vehicle at the end of a long flat landing pad and turned to face Rex. "Mimics are one of the most sophisticated classifications of automatons. They have access to a library of human behavior data. She merely used those tools to offer a genuine performance."

"You never seemed to make use of them."

Todd shook his head. "I failed to value the false comfort they offered." He stepped out of the vehicle and motioned for Rex to do the same. The two leaned against the front of the truck and waited.

A low rumble in the distance caught Rex's attention. He peered across the landing pad and saw only the rippling mirage of the distant horizon reflected in the hard black surface.

Todd pointed into the sky to a spaceship, slow and small in the distance.

As it drew nearer, the rumble grew to a roar until the gently descending stubby-winged vessel seemed to tear the air apart. Its smooth, white skin opened underneath and wheels emerged. Smoke curled, and the wheels screamed as they touched the landing strip. Every movement and minor detail raised more questions in Rex's mind. The underside of the ship separated and descended, creating a ramp lit by electric lights within. Two automatons marched down the ramp carrying an oblong box between them. Though shaped like men, they lacked any detail and their faces bore a pair of lenses and a thin slot for a mouth. Like the ship, their bright white skin seemed smooth, like rubber. As soon as they cleared the ramp they set their payload down and retraced their steps back into the ship.

Rex looked to Todd for approval before he raced to inspect the crate. He ran his hands across the top and edges until he found the mechanism to open it. The box hissed as its seal separated. Rex's mouth hung open and dried out before he regained his senses. Todd strolled up beside him and put a hand on his shoulder.

"I think this'll make her happy," Rex whispered as he fought to catch his breath.

"She has no emotions and no capacity for happiness," Todd argued. "But despite your misguided motives, your plan might at least keep her from pursuing us."

From within the box a replica of Rex sat up. It turned to meet Rex's wide eyed gaze before it climbed out and stood face to face.

Rex frowned. "I couldn't bear to leave her alone. Besides, I think your machine people have feelings and refuse to admit it."

"What gives you that impression?"

Rex circled and inspected his duplicate. "Well, you broke your own rules because you thought it'd be better for me to grow up knowing all these things. Doesn't that sound like an act of love?"

The ship's crew emerged with another oblong box and set it beside the first. Todd opened it and helped his own replica out of its case. He handed his replica a small bag of personal items.

"I merely interpreted my instructions differently than she did."

"How long before she notices that the two people returning from town aren't us?" Rex asked.

"My replica is identical in nearly every way," Todd answered. "Yours..." He went into one of his trances again. "Yours will do just fine."

Rex winced at his father's words. "You're lying, aren't you; lying to save my feelings?"

Todd nodded. "I had intended to end my lying days, but I didn't want you to feel... inadequate in your attempt to protect your mother's feelings."

They watched their doubles climb into the truck and drive back towards town. Rex waved and his replica waved back. Transfixed, he kept his eyes on the vanishing vehicle as he wondered aloud. "Where will we go next?"

Todd tugged at Rex's shoulder and pointed to the rust-colored disk in the sky. "We'll visit all you saw through the telescope firsthand. And when you've had your fill of that, there's a whole galaxy to explore."

Rex looked over to the awaiting ship with its statuesque crew awaiting their orders. "We won't have to ride in those crates, will we?"

"No," Todd answered as he stared into one. Rex couldn't help but wonder if Todd had arrived in the same container a decade ago. He shrugged off a shiver and looked up to the ninety-first Moon with heart fluttering anticipation.

"Then let the adventure begin."

The End

WINFIELD H. STROCK

The Perfect Telescope

Rex followed Todd into a room new to him, the Steward's lair. Its curved walls housed dozens of display panels, each flickered images too quickly for Rex to comprehend. At the room's center, atop a pillar of cables and support beams, sat the Steward of Ninety-First Earth and its solar system. In his throne of luminous chrome, his gunmetal body coursed with veins of muted light. A constellation of stars glowed within ink black hollow eye sockets.

"I understand you wish to pursue your parents," the Steward said, his voice like a cathedral organ, its series of musical notes mimicking the work of lips and a tongue.

Rex took a deep breath and uncringed his shoulders. "Yes."

The Steward shook his head. "That cannot be."

"Are you not built to serve me?" Rex ventured, ashamed of the quiver in his voice.

"I serve humanity, not a single being. Your request threatens pain on those you pursue."

Rex clenched his fists and stomped his foot. "Two years, I've been on this cold rock. I'm tired of having my questions about my parents go unanswered. Why shouldn't they answer for their actions? Why can't I confront them?"

"Questions of 'why' seldom find a satisfactory answer," the Steward replied. He cocked his head. "For example; why did your mimic, Todd, violate the mandate of his makers?"

"Because he saw the harm it was doing to me. That's why he taught me about the Veneer Clause; to protect me from lies and encourage me to explore beyond my fairytale valley."

The Steward stepped down from his throne and loomed over Rex. "I ask myself now, why I don't scrap this malfunctioning mimic, Todd. He's caused more damage than you realize. Your warped attitude threatens a delicate balance within the human-machine civilization."

Rex pulled his gaping mouth shut and swallowed hard. "What do you mean?"

"You value truth over happiness, a dangerous philosophy. You might spread your knowledge and sink your people into a deep depression or worse, violence."

Rex shook his head. "Why would they get violent?"

"Humans turn angry easily and your crusade will demolish what many consider paradise."

"How can I get my answers if you don't let me leave?"

The Steward squatted beside Rex and patted him on the head. He imagined the machine might smile if only he had the features. "Our resources remain at your command to build and enjoy whatever paradise you imagine. Forget this impossible quest for an unnecessary and painful reunion."

Rex's mechanical stepfather, Todd, tugged at his elbow. The boy's audience with the steward ended with him no closer to his goal and no further from his imprisoned life.

****

"This had better work," Rex growled as he stomped back to the telescope's controls.

His stepfather, the mechanical mimic Todd, nodded and replied flatly. "Each new experiment has grown in scope and danger. This one stands to destroy all your work and more should it fail."

Two more years and several failed experiments later, Rex hoped to find his answers from the confines of his prison. The young man sighed. "The containment field's been reinforced after it disintegrated, the new high capacity power couplings shouldn't melt, and I've tightened the warp drive's response tolerances as much as I dare." Rex threw himself into the seat at the telescope's controls, eyed the system's gauges and meters before he forced himself to relax. As he sank into the chair he drew in a long deep breath. He let his hands dangle from the ends of the armrests as he exhaled. Every safety circuit glowed a cool blue on the panel. The needles for coolant pressure, power output, and field intensity all offered assurances his invention remained under control.

A broad screen above showed the center of his invention's focus; a swirling magenta cloud. He chuckled to himself as he pondered the dangers and considered the absence of any safer solution. An implosion of space rather than glimpse through time threatened to cave this corner of the moon in on itself. All the safety circuits stood to naught if he failed to tame time and open a keyhole to his destination.

"You are thinking of halting the experiment?" his stepfather asked, hovering nearby. He placed his gloved hand on Rex's shoulder. "What you seek doesn't warrant risking your life."

"I've been on this moon four years now," Rex replied, "He acts as though my efforts might disturb all I come in contact with, like a virus."

"Machine-kind's stewardship of its creators has eliminated many atrocities born from human conflict," Todd countered. "Your behavior stands to tear down the accomplishments of the Veneer Clause by making others aware of it."

Rex drove his fist into the chair's armrest. "You saved me from a stagnant life."

"In favor of a dangerous one."

Rex grimaced and pulled himself up to the controls. Racing through the sequence to bring all systems to bear on the hazy time-fog, he grumbled, "I'll not come this far without seeing it through."

The cooling systems nearby thrummed to life while the power generator whined into action. Rex watched the time-warp wriggle and fight, wax and wane as he fed it power and bolstered its prison. Feeding and growing, Rex fought to drive its expansion inward, backward through time.

Lightning crackled within the mauve mist as it deepened in color and brightened into a rippling indigo torrent. Rex checked his instruments; the safety circuits fluttered from blue to green and green to yellow. He pushed the controls further, drove his telescope closer toward his goal. The writhing cloud's center dissipated with a pulse of light and a scene lost to history took shape.

Ninety-First Moon's space port appeared, with visiting ships revealing their actions in reverse; landing with the flare of take-off rockets and taking off with sporadic puffs from their retro-thrusters. Rex glanced at the screen's chronometer and accelerated the scope's soar through time. The scene hastened but also jostled out of focus, often losing its view of the landing pad. Rex fought to compensate for the changes in space coordinates, to account for the moon's orbit, the Ninety First Earth's orbit, the star's path through space-time amongst the galaxy. Volumes of data stored by machine-kind across the thousands of worlds provided the positional fixes Rex relied on to calculate this single spot's trajectory through the continuum.

Gradually the landing pad steadied within the view screen. Rex held his breath as one safety circuit skipped past an orange status and glowed red. He looked over his shoulder to Todd. "The cooling system," he shouted. "See what you can do."

With a curt nod Todd raced down the corridor. A second alarm reddened; the containment field. Rex's heart pounded and sweat poured. The containment field's failure endangered everything. From the corridor outside Rex heard rapid footfalls and watched a dozen mechanical men, called Universals, following Todd, running as one. The brigade of machines hurried to halt the burgeoning meltdown.

Rex turned back to his controls and struggled to lessen the stress his scope placed on time and space. But reducing the speed of his probe backwards offered little relief and he realized the truest limitation and danger came from the depth of his efforts. The chronometer indicated thirteen years of travel; three more years to go if his stepfather's story held true. Rex halted his progress and watched operations on the landing pad from long ago unfold at their normal pace, in the proper sequence. He marveled at his success and smiled. All his gauges steadied and status lights settled on yellow.

Todd's voice crackled across the intercom. "The Universals and I made some adjustments and added some last minute augmentations. The system offers seven percent more cooling with a one percent better response time to demands."

"Thanks," Rex replied with a sigh as he reached for the throttle and drove the scope deeper through history. Yellow lights inched to orange across the board as he neared his target. A pair of humans clad in space suits caught his eye as they exited a nearby airlock backwards and strolled toward their ship. Rex centered his scope's focus on the two and followed them into the lunar facility until helmetless faces sent his heart aflutter; his parents.

Rex pushed the scope further and as he watched the ship's arrival, the containment field's alarm reddened. He held the controls steady, halted their backwards progress, and settled the system into a forward progression to see the mystery revealed.

****

His parents exited their ship and marched into the facility. Watching them now trudging forward in their own time, Rex zoomed in on their faces within the suits. His father's bore an angry scowl while red rimmed eyes betrayed his mother's recent tears. A lifetime of living with their mechanical mimics hadn't prepared him to see them so full of emotion, so distraught. Once through the airlock they stripped off their cumbersome suits and marched in silence.

The couple marched into a familiar chilling room; the Steward's lair. At the center of his web of data cables, amidst his planetarium of flickering displays the mechanical titan assessed every corner of his realm.

"How can I help you?" the Steward asked in his melodic voice.

"Can you make duplicates of us to raise our child?" Ann begged. The couple on the screen looked tired, fidgety, and irritable. Todd in particular seemed uneasy with their visit, his eyes darting, searching, and wide with fear while Ann pressed further.

"We can't do it," Ann whimpered as her gaze dropped. "He cries all the time, doesn't sleep when we do, and stinks up the house."

"A nanny might suit your needs," The Steward offered in a soft polite tone. "Mimic attendants can relieve some of the burden."

"It's more than that," Ann muttered as she shot Todd a glare. He turned from her and crossed his arms. Tears streamed down her reddened face. "Todd's a monster and I'll not spend another day with him."

The Steward's attendants, a pair of Universals, entered. Rex shuddered at the eerie, featureless creatures, with their smooth white skin that never wrinkled or stained. They descended on the disheveled pair; one draped a blanket on Ann while the other offered Todd a glass.

"There is a shortage of naturally born infants, especially those raised by their birth parents," the Steward answered with a hint of concern in his voice. "Is there no other way to reconcile this family?"

"I am miserable," Ann shouted.

"Todd?" the Steward asked. "Are you prepared to raise this child? I could fashion a mimic wife as much or as little like Ann as you like."

"Are you kidding?" Todd bellowed. "I've already had enough of this game, especially if Ann gets a pass."

"But the child," the Steward began.

"Enough about him," Todd shouted as he pounded his fist on the table. "I'm an adult, I can speak for myself, and I order you to take this problem away. I don't care how."

Ann collapsed beside him sobbing and wailing.

"I need information," said the Steward. "In order to make proper mimics I must know what memories of your relationship they must have. Otherwise they'll not be convincing. Also I'll need to formulate some questions to ideally understand and comply with your request. Where is the boy?"

"He's asleep in the ship," Ann replied. "The pilot's keeping watch over him."

Rex watched as the attendants ushered Todd out and the door slid shut behind him.

The Steward inched down from his throne with the chilling grace of a spider descending on its prey. Standing seven feet tall, he knelt beside Ann and put his gleaming arm around her. The comforting posture of the inhuman frame made Rex recoil from the scene.

"What do you want for the child?" the Steward asked in a hushed tone.

"People hurt people," she began between sobbing gasps. "I don't ever want that for him. I want him surrounded by love and kindness."

"Tell me about how the two of you met and conceived this child."

"Ever since my nanny told me where babies came from," she began. "I wanted one. I traveled around searching for a man that might agree to a family. I went to the forests on this Earth after a promising message from you." Ann stood, brushed her hair back, and dabbed her tears away. "We courted for a couple of months before he agreed to start a family. After that he turned into a monster."

"What do you mean?" the Steward asked.

"He hated what the baby was doing to my body." She whimpered; then shrugged. "I did too but he was mean about it."

"And after the birth?"

"We fought and fought, before and after. I hadn't expected so much pain or that Rex would need so much maintenance. We commissioned a Universal to take care of things but it kept asking questions and demanding we interact with it."

"You did not love Rex?"

Ann bit her lip and stared at the floor. "I did at first, but it got so hard to enjoy my own life. Todd and I were happier before."

"What would you like your mimic to do that you don't do with respect to Rex?"

"She needs to love him no matter what and to do whatever she can to keep him happy."

Rex watched the woman on the display as she stared back from across sixteen years. Her eyes shifted back and forth and she winced. "Can I go now?"

"Yes."

"Can I be certain I'll never have to face those two again?"

"A wise man once said, 'only uncertainty is certain.' But know that I will do all in my power to protect the three of you."

The curved door slid up as she turned to leave. Before it descended, Todd entered and his scowling face filled the screen.

"She tricked me," he muttered. "She put on her best show, told her best lies, and slapped the trap shut, clamping down on me like a scrap-yard Tasker on a derelict ship."

"What would you like your mimic to do that you didn't do with Rex?"

"Spend time with him without hating it. Teach him things and have patience with him. Oh, and teach him to look out for liars. They'll take hold of your life and drag you down with their schemes."

"And what of later, when he's more mature?"

"What?" Todd blurted as he recoiled. "Get the family back together? I don't want to see Ann ever. As for Rex? Forget it. I don't think we'd hit it off if he knew what I did. I'm just as bad a liar for commissioning a mimic."

Todd's shoulders sagged and a veil of fatigue fell across his features as he turned and shuffled toward the exit.

"Did you not grow up knowing your parents?" the Steward asked.

Without looking back Todd shook his head and answered. "Nope; I was born in a nursery with fifty-one other brats. Our birth mothers slept, never forced to endure the pain of child bearing or the uncomfortable task of raising me. That duty was handled by the farm's handful of nanny mimics."

"Ah, that explains much," the Steward said, his tone hanging in the air like a challenge.

Todd spun around. "What is that supposed to mean?" he growled.

"Nurseries often produce children with behavioral problems due to their mother's comatose condition. Some larger farms have suffered revolt leading to several being shut down or destroyed outright by the children."

Todd's jaw dropped. "Really?"

"We machines understand little about procreation and parenting. It is the reason I worked to preserve your family."

"Maybe next time," Todd quipped with a shrug. "I can't stand to be anywhere near Ann and I'm not going to be left alone with the kid while she struts on out."

A ripple in the image brought Rex's attention to his instruments. Power fluctuations pushed yellow indicators red across the board. He rushed to carefully guide the telescope's energies toward a gradual shutdown. A spike on the gauges and the squeal of metal reverberating in the corridor gave him all the warning he needed. He hit the panic button and the control room's armored door slammed shut from above with the force of a rocket before the warp in space-time imploded. The whole room lurched and tumbled before a hammer blow to the back of his chair drove him into the control console. He felt his limbs turn to rubber and his mind begin to swirl, like water going down the drain until the last of it gurgled into blackness.

****

Pain, distant and muted, awoke Rex. His ribs throbbed in rhythm with his heartbeat. His right eye failed to offer more than a blurry sliver of light when he tried to survey the room. He lay in a bed, propped up at the waist with tubes attached to his arms and wired probes affixed to his chest. Bandage covered arms and legs, though sore, still all responded to his will. As he tests his body's limits, his stepfather leaned into view.

"Hold still, Rex, and rest," Todd whispered. "Your body needs time to heal."

"It worked," Rex laughed until the hammering in his skull bade him stop. "My perfect telescope worked."

"Yes, until it tore itself apart, it did."

Twisting his head as far as he dare, his stepfather remained outside his view. "Where are you? Why are you hiding?"

"I'm behind you," Todd replied. His voice sounded strange, crackling and popping mingled within his words as though speaking through a faulty intercom speaker. "My appearance might be too much for you right now."

"Nonsense," Rex sputtered. "Step forward; I'd rather look at who I'm talking to."

Metal on metal, clicking and hissing, grew louder from over Rex's right shoulder. As Todd stepped into view, Rex's breath caught in his throat. The catastrophe of the time scope stripped the mimic machine's skin from its face. Only Todd's dazzling blue-green eyes remained of features familiar from childhood. At Rex's horrified stare Todd shifted, seemingly searching for a shadow to lessen the shock of his haunting appearance.

"Sorry, Todd," Rex muttered, his voice breaking as he choked back a sob. "I know you're a machine but it still shocks me to see this after a lifetime of knowing you as my dad."

"I warned you."

"Does it hurt?"

Todd shook his head. "I sought to ensure your recovery and the integrity of the facility. I've yet to tend to my superficial damage."

"I'll be fine," Rex said as tears streamed down his cheeks. "Go get yourself fixed up."

With a nod Todd turned to leave. He stopped within the doorway and looked back. "Perhaps instead I should submit myself to destruction."

"Why?" Rex asked with a gasp.

"Your reaction proves the value of the Veneer Clause and our disguised identities. You nearly lost your life pursuing answers to questions I put in your head and I have never seen you more distraught than now. I have failed to adhere to the highest of machine-kind's laws."

"Don't you dare," Rex cried. "I've felt more alive in the years since you opened my eyes. Like these bandages, I felt insulated and restrained by the soft, simple existence my biological parents left me to. More than ever, I need you now."

Todd stared back, his mind locked in another of his expanding moments where the limits of his own mind pushed his thoughts beyond, to the machine network, for answers. "Rest now, I'll return to check on your progress after I've finished my own repairs."

Rex's eyes fluttered shut as his stepfather disappeared behind the silent sliding door.

Todd returned just as Rex awoke. With his appearance and physique fully restored, he greeted the young man with a smile and a tray arrayed with a hearty breakfast. The unique blend of tart citrus and savory aromas melted away the cold artificiality of their abode.

Childhood memories from his woodland home; of the dawn's first rays on his face and the chorus of birds outside his window both lifted Rex's spirits and shadowed him with melancholy.

"You exhibit a strange mixture of emotions," Todd observed. "Why?"

The Veneer Clause: The complete series

"I guess I'm homesick," Rex replied under his breath, still mesmerized by the powerful connection to his blissful past. He shook it off. "So many wonderful memories."

"Further evidence of my faulty logic."

"No," Rex spat back. "Those were the memories of a wonderful childhood you helped create. But I can't remain a naïve child forever. The thought of never growing up, never accomplishing anything, no discovery, no intellectual growth; those awaited me down the path you rescued me from."

A pair of Universals entered the room carrying Rex's learning station, a combination of chair, computer, and personal assistant. Its articulated pieces allowed him uninterrupted study of all that held his interest since he and his stepfather left his home and his stepmother on Ninety-First Earth.

"This proves my point," Rex said as he fought through his pain to point at the Universals' cargo. "Again I see an object that reminds me of wonderful memories."

"This tutorial Tasker?" Todd asked in a near incredulous tone.

Rex chuckled. "Yes, even this. Remember that first year here, how I spent days following scientific subjects from their little beginnings until their expansive end? That's when I hatched the idea of the perfect telescope."

"How?" Todd stepped closer, his eyes transfixed on his stepson.

"Well, remember my star-scope project back home?" After a nod from Todd, Rex continued. "You'd mentioned how it'd been invented before and was called a telescope. I studied the history of the telescope and stumbled on the fact that our perception of stars comes from light shining from so long ago. We were seeing into the past."

Todd shook his head. "Not an entirely accurate statement, but I understand your meaning."

"My obsession with those moments in history, afloat far away; I began my study of interstellar travel. The ships used now warp space-time to reach their destination faster. That's when the two subjects collided and, bam, I began working on how to flip the relationship; to concentrate less on warping space and more on bending time."

Todd and Rex watched the Universals dismantle the tutorial station and work to reassemble it around Rex's bed.

"What will you concentrate on now that you have your answers?" Todd asked.

Rex frowned. "I've found answers but also more questions, questions unanswerable from here."

"I do not like where your statement leads."

Rex looked to Todd and realized the futility of enlisting him as a co-conspirator. "Never mind," he said with a smile. He looked down at himself in bed, hooked up to medical machines. "It'll be awhile before I'm fully recovered. Maybe I'll find some new direction to explore by then."

****

Rex worked hard to recover while Todd kept busy rebuilding the time-bending telescope. From his quarters Rex dove into a myriad of subjects in the library and tinkered with whatever little gadgets his pain-wracked frame could handle. Aside from meals together sharing their thoughts and theories, each pursued their exploits apart for a full year.

Rex grimaced as he leaned against the cane he'd fashioned for himself. Todd's concern revealed itself in his awkward attempts to steady Rex when the cane's necessity became apparent. Rex reached out and clutched his stepfather's hand and squeezed. "You can't see it, can you?"

Todd scanned Rex and the room around them.

With chuckle, shaking his head, Rex explained. "You claim machines lack emotion and yet you behavior says otherwise."

The two walked in silence through corridors until Rex stopped with a gasp within the threshold of the rebuilt time-telescope facility.

"What's this?" Rex muttered. He pursed his lips tight before continuing. "This isn't my telescope."

"I only rebuilt with care what you invented in haste," Todd replied flatly as he examined his stepson's reaction. "Many well-documented engineering concepts crossed my mind as I began recreating your work."

Rex laughed until a true danger caught his next breath. "Did you involve the Steward?"

"I used all information available," Todd answered. His brow tightened a millimeter. "The Steward monitors my path through the data stream." He offered a slight shrug. "We cannot access the library beneath his notice."

Rex winced before he forced a chuckle. "It's alright; I've proven my point with the telescope. Now all I need is an audience with him, to convince him."

Todd frowned a fraction. "I do not understand."

Shaking his head, Rex smiled. "The less you know; the better."

"Judging from your last experiment," Todd countered. "I have my doubts."

"Just see to it I have an audience with the Steward soon; my telescope has its limits and I must act fast to see what I'm after before it slips out of sight."

****

Rex limped beside his stepfather until they stood at the curved threshold of the Steward's lair. As the door slid up before them, Rex stamped his shining steel cane against the floor.

"Stay outside," he insisted. "This fight I must face alone."

Todd hesitated a millisecond. "Stay focused on your goal and don't let your temper interrupt your train of thought."

Rex sighed. "Thanks, but I'll be alright. You stay right here just in case things get out of hand."

Todd nodded, frowning.

The door slid shut behind him with a hushed click as Rex approached the Steward's throne. The flickering data screens no longer fascinated Rex; they agitated him. With each hobbling step closer his gaze tilted higher to behold his jailor atop his glittering throne.

"Your stepfather has rebuilt your dangerous toy," the Steward said, his melodic voice heavy with disdain. "Have you not seen enough? Have you not come close enough to death to recoil from another such encounter?"

Rex winced as he straightened himself and drew in a deep breath. "I've seen all I can."

"Good," the Steward said. "Whatever else you require-

"You didn't let me finish," Rex spat back. "I've seen all I can from here. Now my telescope and I must travel to those places in space closer to the coordinates in time I plan to bring into view next."

"I do not follow," the Steward said, his vocal notes sounded off key, jagged.

Rex hobbled closer, leaning more on his cane as he hastened his pace. "Only by positioning myself directly over the point in space I want to observe can I get closer to my target observation in space-time."

The chamber door hissed open behind Rex as the Steward gestured for him to leave with a dismissive wave of his hand. "You're a danger to your fellow humans and I suspect your quest for answers will not end until you've disrupted the lives of your parents and all in your path."

Rex lifted his cane and pointed at the Steward, thrusting it closer with every syllable as he spoke. "Machines farmed my father from a crop of embryos, borne by unconscious women, and raised by mechanical nannies. You admitted fault in that process and yet you lock me away because I seek the truth and to hold my parents accountable for their absence? How dare you claim to understand the danger I represent!"

"We have tried everything we know," the Steward conceded. His voice raised an octave as he responded further. "I brought your parents together myself. When Ann expressed an interest in bearing a child and finding a suitable husband, I convinced their ships to come here. I orchestrated their chance encounter. They seemed suitable, satisfied. Why can't humans stand their own kind?"

"You've given them an easier alternative, a life surrounded by admirers and slaves."

"But humanity's fading, their numbers fall daily."

"Maybe by sharing the truth I can sour people on their false paradise," Rex pleaded.

"I cannot defy my programming for your selfish and flimsy hypothesis," the Steward replied. "I must do what I consider best." He inched a finger out until he pushed the accusatory cane aside. As he did so, Rex activated a switch hidden within his cane. A shimmering pulse thrummed from the gleaming rod and rippled out to the surrounding walls. The Steward stumbled from his throne and fell to the grated floor at Rex's feet. The flickering data-streaming screens all went blank.

"It's my life," Rex growled as he towered over the fallen Steward. "I'll do what I want." He turned to the exit and ran to Todd. "We've got to get out of here, now."

"Your limp," Todd muttered. "What happened?"

"I needed an excuse to enter the Steward's chamber armed," Rex said with a smile. "Now we must act quickly to escape."

Todd froze, his eyes distant.

"Don't seize up on me now!" Rex screamed before he realized what must happen. "If we don't leave now I'll die of madness."

Todd scooped Rex up in his arms and ran faster than ever before. Through spacious corridors designed for the Taskers, his racing footfalls echoed. As the spaceport's airlock loomed larger, a pair of Universals emerged from an adjoining passage. Rex's fearful cry caught in his throat as he discerned their purpose. Todd's concern for Rex's life had turned the prison's guards into allies.

Each carried a spacesuit and began dressing them both as they reached the small armored exit. But before they finished, an unspoken command paralyzed them. Rex's helmet hovered in the Universal's hands above his head. As he plucked down the helmet and fastened it to his suit Rex looked to Todd. His stepfather shoved past their attendants, tore open the airlock's control panel and overrode the interior door open. Rex ran into the airlock after him.

"What about your helmet?" Rex asked as he held his hand ready to lower his face-shield.

"I don't really need it," Todd replied as he commanded the inner door shut and nodded for his stepson to seal his suit. As he did so, Todd worked the airlock's controls again. Rex reached down to where his stepfather's helmet spun like a top on the airlock floor, snatched it up and clamped it into place. Air hissed through the vents as massive vacuum pumps reclaimed the precious gases. Rex noticed the noises around him thin out until only his breathing, heartbeat, and the whir of the suit's machinery remained. With a hushed click the outer door opened and the emptiness of space devoured what remained of the air and dust particles within the chamber.

Rex raced past two large cargo ships. He'd studied each ship that arrived over the years and learned which were designed for human occupancy. He ran to a small courier ship on the edge of the landing pad as a stuttering sputtering broken melody crackled inside his helmet. The notes sounded clipped, stretched, and repeated over and over. A clearer voice came through as he fumbled with the ships outer hatch.

"We must hurry," Todd's tinny voice insisted. "The Steward's back-up systems are restoring him. There's no telling when he'll be back on line, but from the sound of it, soon."

Together they forced the hatch open and dove in. Todd clamored for the atmospheric systems while Rex climbed into the pilot's chair to lock out all external access. He thanked the generations before him, insisting on a degree of human habitability amongst the machine fleet. To suit their whimsical masters most ships carried living quarters and ample supplies to last a small contingent until the next star.

As air roared in from storage tanks, a winking light on the communications console startled Rex. He raced through the take-off sequence he'd memorized in the final days of his recovery. Engines whined and landing gear groaned as the ship lurched from the launch pad only to fall back down with a resounding rumble. A cascade of warning lights flashed while each system fell silent save the chug and whir of the life support systems. Each alarm blinked out until only the communications prompt and the navigation error alarm remained.

Rex flipped on the radio. "Let me go!" he screamed.

A melodic reply chilled his spine. "You must stay, I insist."

"Stop me and you'll kill me," Rex spat back. "Is that what you want?"

"Your empty threat prompted a simple mimic to acquiesce but I know better. Madness will not end your life."

Rex chuckled. "It does when you give a madman access to the destructive force of my telescope."

"What do you mean?"

"I've set my perfect telescope to automatically begin a probe through time to the dawn of mankind."

"Your device lacks the power for so deep a search," the Steward said with an inquisitive inflexion.

"And what do you think will happen in the attempt?"

"Your telescope will shut down."

"That presumes all the safety circuits are still working," Rex said managing as much bravado as he dare. "They are not. In fact, soon Ninety-First Moon will suffer a catastrophic event even you cannot survive." Sweat trickled down his ribs within the spacesuit as he eyed the ship's chronometer.

"Why?" the Steward asked.

"Escaping your prison wouldn't be enough," Rex answered while he fought to regain control of his ship. "I can't have you warning other worlds with your twisted vision of the threat I represent."

The engines shuddered to life and the navigational charts flickered onto the display. Rex drove the ship upward as fast as he dared.

"I am proud," the Steward said with a hint of warmth in his voice. "You will see my vision fulfilled."

"What?" Rex asked.

"Conflict is a catalyst for change," the Steward answered. "My efforts to engineer a family failed but your stepfather was my great triumph. In building mimics on par with myself, I created the perfect blend of opposing opinions on how to raise you. Their conflict exposed a fault within the Veneer Clause. When I noticed the effect on your development and aggressive attitude toward your principles, I chose the most constrictive logical path to evaluate your danger to humanity. I became your enemy so that you might fight to destroy a way of life I was created to protect."

Rex's heart skipped a beat and his next breath caught in his throat. Not since he escaped his stepmother, the love smothering machine, had he felt so strong a pang of remorse. He flipped one screen's display until the moon appeared; shrinking behind them. He turned a knob to zoom in and beheld the rust colored patchwork of old factories. From the pixelated horizon, a distortion of light caught his eye. A long shining new tunnel extended out to a cluster of shimmering buildings; the telescope facility Todd rebuilt.

The pinpoints of light, stars above that distant horizon, smeared downward until they looked like icicles in the sun. Their brilliant clarity blurred as though seen through a deformed glass lens. The facility's roof smoldered from within and buckled in an instant. Bright flashes erupted only to be sucked inward to the whirlpool's center as the surrounding landscape folded and crumbled into a rapid landslide towards an expanding darkness at its epicenter. Then a sudden shudder and ripple of the image startled Rex as he felt the ship shake in the wake of the temporal tsunami. He checked his instruments. Aside from a brief flash of red across all circuits the ship thrummed on through space, its course unaltered, its hull intact. He looked back at the rear-facing screen and gasped. A deep wound pierced Ninety-First Moon; its jagged edges encompassed half the Steward's realm and sank into blackness.

"You deceived me," Todd said, "and destroyed much."

"I had no choice," Rex replied. "You couldn't have kept a secret if you tried."

"I rebuilt your telescope to help you better see your past."

A nervous laugh caught Rex by surprise as he pondered the details of his escape. "Ironic, isn't it?"

"I don't follow," Todd responded.

"That I used an instrument for viewing the past to secure my future."

The End

Zealot's Folly

"Do you realize how few children get to know their parents?" Rex asked.

Ian nodded. "With good reason, I guess. I mean, we're not easy to get along with. Why else have mimics?"

Rex shifted in his chair. The room felt ten degrees warmer. "You mean you approve of your abandonment?"

Ian scowled as he recoiled from the question. "I wouldn't call it that." His features softened and he smiled. "They saved me from the fighting and crying that comes from human companionship." He chuckled. "Do I look abandoned and forlorn?" He held out his hands and gestured to their surroundings.

In Ian's spacious home, they sat in a circle of oversized plush chairs. Servants, perfectly sculpted mimics, hovered within arm's reach, anxious to offer food, drink, and more. These seductive constructs represented the full pantheon of Ian's lascivious tastes, from thin to voluptuous, men and women, athletic and obese. Rex found his mind and body at odds, revulsion and temptation warring each time they glided nearby to refresh his drink or replenish his empty plate.

Before Rex answered, Todd extended his hand and shook Ian's. "Thank you, you've given us what we're looking for." Todd stood and put a hand on Rex's shoulder. The young man stiffened at his foster father's touch.

"Don't you care? Don't you care that your life is a meaningless, purposeless, waste?" Rex fumed.

Ian shrugged. "See, this is what I'm talking about. I play the perfect host and you sour an afternoon with nonsense," Ian motioned for his servants to escort them out. "Humans can only stand each other if there's sex involved, and even then only for a little while."

Todd's fingers pressed harder into Rex's shoulder. "We should go now, Rex. Our questions have been answered and our host has other interests to entertain."

Rex rose and Todd tugged at him as he headed toward the exit.

"Whatever you're doing," Ian yelled as they retreated, "don't disturb my little corner of paradise with your... whatever."

Rex turned to follow Todd and marched out to the nearby landing pad.

"How can he live like that?" Rex asked as he stepped up the ramp, into their ship.

"Machines have catered to humanity's desires for millennia," Todd answered. "We were designed to ease suffering and build paradise. As difficult as it may be to accept, even your parents held your happiness in mind when they commissioned me and your surrogate mother to be built and take their place."

"That's not what I mean," Rex grumbled with a dismissive wave. "You saw how he ate, all those sweets and meat. How is he not a blubbery mess?"

"Metabolizers," Todd replied. "Nanites, microscopic taskers ingested regularly. They adjust metabolism, condition muscle tissue, and alter digestive processes to maintain a healthy body."

Rex jerked back, eyes wide. "Little automatons inside you?"

"They are perfectly harmless," Todd explained. "No ill side effects have been noted in the centuries they've been employed within billions of humans."

"But, what else do they do besides keep you healthy?" Rex wondered. He gasped. "Have I been infected with those things?"

Todd's features froze. Impatient for an answer, Rex offered a clarifying statement. "I know it'll upset me to know, but I want to know. Have I had those things in me?"

After a moment's confusion, Todd nodded. "We kept you on a healthy diet but as a precaution we've had metabolizers administered to you your whole life."

"If I've eaten healthy, why else have me take them?"

"They can also be programed to examine for and eliminate many debilitating ailments. They find aberrant mutated cells and isolate them."

"Oh."

The ship's soft feminine voice cautioned them to buckle in as the whine of the engines outside deepened to a deafening roar. Ian's sprawling mansion shrank in the window, vanishing as the ship veered toward their destination, another orphan of apathy.

"How long before the machines catch on?" Rex wondered. "How long before they reject the idea that I've installed you as the acting steward of Ninety-First Earth?"

After a moment's introspection, Todd answered. "They have yet to make any judgment concerning your destruction of the previous steward. Tranquility and productivity influence them most."

"I would've thought my actions threw tranquility out the window," Rex said shaking his head. "I know I spent the first couple days afterward planning an escape."

"And yet, in this world without a steward, you find the freedom to... execute your plan." Todd's gaze sharpened. "What is your plan? What is your goal exactly?"

After the ship steadied on course, she invited them to enjoy refreshments during the hour's journey. Rex unbuckled himself, grabbed a tall glass of apple juice, and strolled to the viewing window spanning the lower half of the aft bulkhead. The arboreal wilderness rolling beneath seemed strange to Rex. Sixteen years of life amidst the verdant valley, all those memories, seemed stolen from a child Rex knew in a dream. After four years of life on the Moon, in its controlled atmosphere and industrial environment, he yearned for those days when the mimic beside him *was* his father as far as he knew and they discovered the stars together.

Rex sighed. "Should comfort and pleasant distraction be life enough?" He reached out and pulled the glove from Todd's left hand, revealing the mimic's wire sinews and steel skeletal frame. "You exposed me to the sham so I might live a fulfilling life probing the unasked questions of this crazy universe. I want to excite people, get them passionate about the exploration of themselves, new ideas, and the worlds around them."

Todd allowed a brief frown. "Your purpose may run contrary to my own."

"How so?" Rex asked aghast. He threw Todd's glove to the floor. "You freed me. Why reverse your philosophy and oppose my crusade to free everyone else?"

"As your father I took what actions that responsibility demanded. As appointed steward, my concern for you must be weighed against the tranquility of all this world's inhabitants."

Rex nodded. "That's why I've begun with a careful line of questioning. You taught me to feel them out, to assess whether they're ready for such a big step."

Todd's response came slowly, concern darkened his countenance. "You *must* be sure or else you risk harm."

"I'll do my best," Rex replied with a weak smile. "Were you sure?"

Todd frowned a fraction. "Something must've corrupted my memory," Todd began as his eyes darted from side to side as if reading the information as he spoke. With a blink he set aside the phantom document. "Statistical data from that moment appear less favorable now than they did then."

"So, what's that mean?" Rex asked.

"I'm not sure."

Rex returned his attention to the world below as the ship shuddered and shifted. Ribbons of white and grey fluttered and faded as they cut through the clouds. Rivulets streaked across the window. Between the clouds and through the trickling rain, Rex beheld orderly rows of pale green cabbage, amber shocks of wheat, and wispy topped stalks of corn.

Rain hissed and spattered as the ship's hatch yawned open, its upper portion offering shelter and the bottom extended as a ramp. Rex pulled his raincoat collar up, his broad-brimmed hat down, and stepped onto the farm's landing pad. Over his shoulder he watched Todd stroll, unphased by the chilling downpour and unblinking as the droplets drizzled down his face.

They trudged along a cobblestone path, laser straight through a canyon of corn. Movement caught Rex's eye, sporadic and scattered amongst the stalks. He halted, craned his neck, and found the culprits. Tall lanky taskers tiptoed through the rows. With a gentle touch and eyes atop prehensile tendrils, they examined their crop. Like enormous alien insects, they wore hard exoskeletons adorned in a camouflage color scheme.

The tall house dwarfed Rex's childhood home and sported a large porch around its base covered by an awning of metal that rang with the din of the rain. To the right Rex noticed a porch swing rocking lazily in the protected shade.

He crept up the stairs and peered down upon the swing's occupant, a woman.

A midnight river of thick, wavy hair framed her angel face and cascaded down the sun baked, smooth skin of her bare neck and shoulders. Rex's heart skipped a beat as he noticed a detail in the depths of her profile he'd never seen before, her pulse thrumming as she slept. She lay dressed in dirt-caked clothes, clutching her blanket with work-worn hands. Rex noticed a dripping raincoat and muddy boots next to the swing.

Todd leaned close and whispered, "Her name is Sara."

Rex nodded as he continued to watch her sleep. Distant thunder rumbled and she slowly opened her eyes. Closing them again, she stretched her arms and legs out as she strained to shake the remnants of her slumber. Only after she sat up and opened her eyes again, she noticed Rex. She leaned back and blinked, her eyes growing wider.

"Oh, hello," she said. "Who are you?"

A moment passed before Rex regained his senses, realized he'd been asked a question, and answered. "Um, I'm Rex and this is Todd. We're visiting folks, getting to know them. Do you mind?"

Sara ran her hands through her hair, rubbing her scalp vigorously. She yawned and turned her head until her neck popped, turning her wince into a smile. "I don't guess I mind. It's odd though. I don't get visitors often, except mom and dad."

"You know your parents?" Rex asked.

"Well, yeah." Sara stood, motioned for Rex to follow, and strolled into the big house.

The home displayed many of the rustic elements of Rex's childhood home: a fireplace, wood-burning stove, roughhewn furniture, and simple kitchen utensils. But bits of technology littered the simple setting, and occasional conveniences were sprinkled throughout.

Sara walked into the kitchen, muttered to a compact machine in the corner, and withdrew a steaming pitcher from it. She motioned for them to sit as she fetched a couple of cups and poured Rex and Todd each a drink. After she got herself a cup, she sat across from them.

Rex looked at the dark, steaming drink and sniffed. Mildly acidic, it smelled a bit like the freshest, darkest dirt his mother used in her garden. Though the nostalgic aroma comforted him, he hardly imagined the liquid suitable sustenance.

Todd pushed aside the cup offered him. "I'm sorry, I don't drink coffee."

Sara shrugged. "Suit yourself. I need a big cup after a good long nap."

Rex brought the cup to his lips and tipped it up only enough to catch a small sip. Hot and bitter, he recoiled from it and ran his tongue across the roof of his mouth.

Sara laughed. "I don't guess either of you drink coffee."

Rex felt his face flush and his palms sweat. He forced a chuckle. "Nonsense, it's just that I... uh... ate something that didn't agree with the flavor." He tilted his head back and took in a mouthful of the hot, bitter, nasty stuff. After struggling to choke it down he grinned. "That's better."

Again Sara laughed. She laughed until her face reddened, her eyes glistened with tears, and she stopped only to regain her breath. "I haven't laughed like that in ages," she said after a long sigh.

Rex frowned and fidgeted with his half empty mug. "So, about your parents, you know them and they visit you?"

Sara mimicked Rex's serious posture and furrowed brow. She clenched her fists on the table and responded in a deep voice, "I knew them and they visited." She relaxed and continued. "It's been a long time, ever since they left me in charge of the farm."

"They used to live here, together, on the farm with you?" Rex asked, leaning closer.

"Well, sure, at some point I suppose, but they'd moved to separate homes nearby before I can remember. They took turns living here with me. Mom explained how men and women come together to make babies, but that they can't stay together because people are so different and too difficult to be around for any length of time before they fight."

"So they raised you by taking turns throughout the years?"

Sara nodded. "The steward recommended the arrangement. Mom told me about how important he'd made it sound, spending time with little ol' me as I grew up. Sometimes they'd leave me with a nanny machine, when I was particularly difficult. Dad showed me how to run the farm most of the time and Mom tried to teach me how to play tennis." Sara's gaze grew distant and she slowly shook her head. "I never got the knack for it. It made her so angry I didn't enjoy it… or ever get any better."

"Do they contact you any these days?" Rex wondered.

"Mom and I don't like each other enough for that," Sara said, frowning. As her features relaxed her gaze grew distant again. "And Dad, he's another story." A weak smile emerged. "We had so much fun out in the fields, watching the crops grow and knowing how we made other people happy with our harvest." The smile faded and her voice dropped to a murmur. "But one day there was an accident. Lightning struck one of the taskers out in the field and fried its mind. We didn't know until we were out checking on the damage left by the storm. The tasker went berserk when we tried to shut it down. It tore my dad to pieces."

"Oh my," Rex exclaimed. "That sounds horrible."

A nervous laugh escaped Sara as she met Rex's startled stare. She wiped her watering eyes. "It wasn't so bad, he wasn't really my father. He'd skipped out years ago and left a mimic to raise me."

"You too?"

She batted her eyes. "Yeah, I guess my mom knew what she was talking about. People can't stand people."

"But, don't you think maybe we should learn?" Rex asked. "Don't you think people must've, at one time, been able to cooperate, converse, and coexist?"

"Well, sure, in the days before mimics." She flashed a smile. "But now everyone's free to enjoy their lives completely. With no arguments or clashing egos, no jealousy or resentment, we can all focus on the positives every moment of every day."

Rex held up his cup. "When I nearly scalded my throat and choked on this disgusting drink, you laughed, you laughed harder than you had in ages."

Sara snickered. "Yeah, that was pretty funny."

"No machine has made you laugh that hard?" he ventured.

While the smile remained, her eyes darkened. "No."

Rex pointed to the fields outside. "The tragedy of losing your father in that accident, didn't the anguish of it diminish when you realized it was a copy of your father and not the real man you'd grown up loving?"

Sara hurled her cup past him and screamed. "NO! When he cheated Mom and I, when he left without ever saying goodbye, that's the greatest pain I've ever felt." Sara buried her reddened face into her hands and sobbed. "Mom screamed at me when she found out, she screamed and then she cried. That was the last time I ever saw her."

The room grew quiet. Even the rhythmic drumming of the rain upon the roof faded. Only the drip-drip-drip of the storm's remains interjected in the expanding silence. Rex felt a firm grasp on his shoulder. He looked up to see Todd, Sara's undamaged cup in his hand. Gently he set the cup down between the two screaming humans.

"We should go now," Todd said. "We've upset Sara and that was not our intent."

"Yes, go," Sara whimpered, her voice trembling. "I don't know why you came, I don't know why you said those things, all I know is I don't want you to ever visit me again."

Rex leaned closer. Todd grabbed him by the shoulders and pulled him to his feet. Rex shook free and pleaded with Sara.

"I only wanted to open your eyes to the folly of the false lives we're all living. Humanity's falling apart because we're insulating ourselves, isolating ourselves from the one thing we must embrace- each other."

"You idiot!" she screamed as she stood, fists clenched, arms stiff by her sides. "Your visit has been a perfect example of why my parents and yours left. Somebody says something horrible or does something selfish sooner or later."

"That's not what I'm doing," he countered. "I'm trying to restore humanity. I'm trying to explain how much richer and fulfilling our lives can be."

Todd reasserted his grip. Rex felt himself pulled backwards as he spoke his final words. He heard the door swing open behind him and Todd spun him around in time to step down off the porch and began the long walk back to the landing pad. The sun peeked through the dispersing clouds and revealed the shining wetness of the surrounding foliage. Steam hugged the road and rolled over the tall walls of corn. Without the rain to mask their movements, Rex heard the taskers nearby and looked. While a pair worked side by side in a row near the cobblestone path he thought one kept a wary eyestalk on him as he passed by.

Once Rex and Todd crested the rolling hillside at the landing pad's edge, the ship came to life. Its hatch opened and the pre-takeoff whir of the engines began to purr. Stepping up the ship's brow Rex hesitated and turned to take in the vibrant colors of a lively world before he returned to his home of stone and steel on the moon. The potpourri of scents, fresh rain, tilled earth, and the pollen of a hundred different plants simultaneously thrilled and pained him. The childhood memories, the shocking truth, and his recent debacle he'd envisioned as his first step toward an enlightened world.

Amidst his woolgathering, a bobbing head of a jogging figure startled him, a universal. The automaton's colors matched the greens and browns of farm life. It raced toward the ship with a small package in its plastic coated hands. It slowed as it drew near and held up the tiny parcel, an offering to Rex. The machine's featureless face still managed to condemn his actions and look at him with an invisible scorn. The voice jolted him. It was Sara's in a recorded message.

"Take this cup. I don't want any reminders of your visit and I want you to remember how hurtful you were before you ever again try to open anyone else's eyes."

Rex took the cup and thanked the universal. He watched the machine race up the nearby slope until it disappeared before letting his fingers slip from the memento, dropping it to the landing pad with a crash. He trudged into the ship and collapsed onto his seat. At the ship's insistence, he buckled himself in.

The soft whir of the engines rose in pitch and volume until it sounded like a persistent scream after the hatch clamped shut. The scream gave rise to a roar and the vessel drove up and veered away as a fresh clump of rain clouds crawled over the horizon.

****

"Rex, you've been secluded in your private quarters for a week now." Todd's message sounded loud and angry, an illusion no doubt created by the absence of any voices during his solitary stint. "Please contact me soon, we should talk about recent events and how they may reshape your future."

Rex had searched a galaxy of music in the database and found nothing to soothe his tortured heart, nothing to raise his sunken spirits. In his darkest moments alone he'd sought a dirge to commiserate with but either machine-kind had purged such disdainful music from the library or humanity's sorrowful soul had never sought such solace.

The message had been sent a day or two ago, Rex's sense of time lacked any point of reference. Only his unshaven face and un-bathed odor reminded him occasionally of the distant tick of a clock. He pressed a button on his data console and sent his reply. "Let's have dinner tonight."

On the outer edge of the factory complex rebuilt after the steward's demise, Rex had erected a new and separate structure, a home and fortress equipped to afford Rex more autonomy and less surveillance than he'd previously known. Only a narrow causeway connected the self-sufficient building to the rest of the lunar facility. It housed its own spaceport and Rex fashioned his own staff of universals and taskers, separate from the networked population. Atop this thin stretch of metal sat the dining room where he and Todd had celebrated many milestones since that first victory. Now Rex dreaded the meal and what his mimic stepfather might propose in light of recent failures.

Rex entered the empty dining room, shocked. Todd's punctuality never failed until now, and the absence of their dinner staff mechanical attendants also sent his mind spiraling into paranoia.

The machines, they've sent a replacement steward during my absence and this dinner invitation means nothing more than a trap. I've prepared my personal quarters for this moment only to be lured out by the only machine I trust.

But before his retreat began, the doors across the hall opened. Sara and a pair of universals entered. The universals each carried their typical trays laden with the evening's meal. Sara remained close to the entrance, waiting while the machines set the table. As they departed, Todd entered and escorted Sara in. Only then Rex realized the table he and Todd had dined at had been modified for three place settings.

"I assumed you'd willingly allow Sara to dine with us," Todd said after a shallow bow.

"B-b-but of course," Rex managed. "How though? How is it you're here? I mean, it's great but I just don't... I didn't..."

Sara giggled. "You managed to make me laugh again. I didn't think that possible." She cleared her throat and regained her composure. With a meager smile she continued. "I got to thinking about what you said after you left. There's more to life, isn't there?"

Rex felt aglow and his vision blurred as tears welled up. He brushed them aside, reached out and grasped her hand. "Yes, Sara, humanity's been living the life of a parasite. We've created a host and we're merely hanging on. I've ached to share my dream with someone, to find a partner to embrace my crusade with me."

She cast her gaze on their intertwined fingers. "I don't know what all that is, but I'm willing to have dinner with you. Todd invited me up to make peace and see the kind of wonders you two have up here."

"Perhaps you two should eat soon," Todd interjected. "Humans tend to become less pleasant as hunger sets in."

Rex and Sara chuckled before they dove into their meals. All three ate in silence until Rex stopped, set his fork down, and apologized. "Sara, I'm sorry I upset you. I got so adamant about changing your mind I didn't consider how horrible those memories must've been."

"I felt I had to give you a second chance," she conceded with a smile. "We started so well."

Even Todd managed a fraction of a smile. "When you locked yourself away, I felt I had to do something. I pleaded with Sara to come."

After their dinner, the three strolled around the lunar complex. Rex explained what he could while Todd explained the rest. Rex shared the story of the Steward, the telescope, and his mimic parents. Sara shared little more than she'd already told them about her upbringing and her favorite details about the farm. Near the end of their tour, Todd excused himself.

Rex and Sara returned to the dining hall. He'd designed it for an ideal, unobstructed view of Ninety-First Earth. They looked out across a rust colored desert where the world of greens and blue hung in the sky, framed by stars, unblinking in the vacuum of space. Clouds streaked the azure globe Rex loved to watch as it rolled lazily through time.

"Now that we've visited each other's homes, we can consider each other friends, I guess," Sara offered with a shy smile.

Rex's eyes lit up. "You haven't even seen my home yet." He reached out and took Sara's hand. "I've built my own separate home apart from the factory and spaceport." Briskly, he strode to the other end of the hall and entered a code into the door's keypad. "I've designed the entire suite to be machine-proof, in case they ever try to imprison me again."

He took her through halls, to rooms, and showed her equipment, all a hodge-podge of current and older technology blended with unique pieces. The facilities were staffed by Rex's own, modified mechanical men. They functioned like universals, but lacked the smooth rubbery outer skin that had always made Rex uneasy. Opposite the dining hall and passageway to the factories, Rex showed her his private spaceport and his specially outfitted ship.

"The steward tried to stop me by severing my tie to the navigational network," he said excitedly. "Here I've created my own, self-updating, navigational computer. With this ship I can go anywhere without any interference."

"You seem certain they'll try and stop you," Sara observed.

"The consequences of being unprepared, and the years before when the steward kept me captive, pushed me pretty hard to get all this done."

She nodded as she took the whole room in. "Looks like you've thought of everything."

Rex grinned before he raced to a squat armored cabinet. "You haven't seen my secret weapon. It's not fully functional yet." He opened the top and threw a switch. Two antennae rose from the sides and a colorful display glided out from the front. A wriggling blue waveform danced across a dull green screen.

"It's designed to scramble the steward and his machines," Rex said. "Right now it only has a limited range, but once I get it tied into some of my other equipment I'll be able to shut down anything I don't want working across the entire moon."

Rex jumped as something large fell nearby. He spun around to see Sara on the floor, convulsing. Her eyes fluttered and her body twitched. She uttered a strange repetitive sound. Whatever happened, her muscles drew tight all over. He ran to his communications console to call for a medic before he realized his mistake. Instead of calling for a doctor, he raced to the gadget he'd been showing her and switched it off. Sara's seizures stopped.

An alarm sounded throughout his fortress home. An intruder. He raced to his desk and directed the defense of his home, dispatching loyal machines to key points, locking down all routes but his escape to the ship. Cameras flickered from scene to scene until the culprit came into focus on the big central screen. Todd. He dodged and disabled defenders as he fought his way inward. With surprising agility and ferocity he cut through each obstacle and guardian until sheer numbers forced him to the floor and bound him with their hands of iron.

After Rex checked the skies and double checked the rest of the facility he marched within a ring of bodyguards to meet Todd. Sara had not moved since her convulsions had stopped. Rex left guards there just in case. Close at hand, he carried the electrostatic cane he'd built to defeat the steward, nervously turning it over and over in his hands.

"What is the meaning of this," he demanded.

Todd looked up from the swarm of machine-men holding him. "Of all the human emotions you've suspected me of, I've experienced regret the most."

"What have you done?" Rex screamed. "Why?"

"To answer your questions in reverse order," Todd began. "I saw your pain, your sadness, and I had to act. When my attempts to broker a peace with Sara failed, I commissioned a mimic to ease your suffering."

"But you know how much I despise the lies."

"And yet you have largely considered me your father, an equal, a human being from the beginning of our adventures because you crave human companionship; unlikely, until you convert at least one person to your cause."

Rex dismissed the guards surrounding them both and closed to help Todd up. The mimic looked to Rex's hand and his own. But before he accepted it, Todd peeled away the glove he'd worn since the day he revealed to Rex the truth behind his idyllic childhood. Only then, with his fingers of wire muscles and steel bones, did he accept Rex's help and stand.

"I've grown into adulthood and yet I've held onto childish notions," Rex observed, his eyes transfixed on the two hands grasping each other. "You don't have emotions, do you?"

"Only algorithms designed to emulate them and a library of psychological data."

"I kept thinking you were on the verge of having your own true emotions."

"I hope that never happens," Todd said. "They put logic on unsteady ground and drive people to unwise action."

A nervous laugh escaped Rex, a laugh that devolved into a broken sob. "I'm more alone than I've been willing to admit." He pursed his lips and fought back the burgeoning tears. "Am I wrong in this crusade of mine?"

Todd's head tilted. "Strange that the first to call you pursuit of truth a crusade was the Steward, who saw in you his own destruction, a violation of his programming, and yet welcomed both." He straightened himself and offered a curt nod. "If his logic and your heart draw the same conclusion, how else can it be wrong?"

****

Rex locked Todd in place atop the operating table and retreated to the controls. "I can't help feeling bad for what I'm about to do," he said. "And yet there's no other way I can get past my childhood."

Without looking up, Todd replied with his usual calm. "I agree with your decision and own no ego to bruise. My mutilation seems an ideal means eradicate the final deception before you. No more lies between us, even the lie that protected you from loneliness."

Rex pulled back on the control panel's lever and released a shower of acid. Harmless to humans, the liquid blackened and crisped Todd's skin as it oozed down his naked body. Tendrils of smoke curled up from the expanding cracks in Todd's faux flesh.

Apple juice, Rex had been told once, the glass he held contained apple juice. It had been Todd's trick, his stepfather's gambit to free the boy he called son for fourteen years. With that shattered cup, Rex had watched his mother melt before him and his simple life fall away.

Todd held still as the acid drenched him, except that he followed its decent, he watched it consume him. With a gentle approving nod, he acknowledged the complete erasure of his disguise and with a sudden, violent shudder, he shook off the charred remnant.

"This will be better now," Todd conceded. "Now we can work together knowing fully where our relationship stands."

Rex felt his throat go dry and his eyes moisten. He swallowed and took in a deep breath before he approached the gleaming machine he'd called "father". The pungent aroma and wisps of smoke clung to his nostrils and felt thick within his lungs. With a few shallow coughs he fought to clear the offending film. Inches from Todd, he looked into the only familiar feature remaining, his brilliant green eyes set within a cold steel skull. A chill rippled down Rex's spine.

"I am sorry," Rex said, his voice weak and uneven.

Todd shook his head as his wiry sinews attempted a smile. "I've told you, there's no reason for remorse. I understand your actions and accepted this task."

Rex dropped his gaze to the floor between them before he found the courage to continue. "You don't understand, Todd. I'm not done."

Todd tilted his head as he wondered aloud. "What do you mean? What else stands between us?"

Rex cleared his throat before he spoke again. "Protocol, reveal."

From the center of Todd's head, a piston protruded which Rex grasped and turned over in his hands.

"What are you doing?" Todd asked, his tone urgent, almost panicked. "You could've found easier ways to destroy me. What are you doing?"

Rex looked up from the core in his hand as he withdrew a small data chip from his vest pocket.

"You asked what else stands between us," Rex answered. "The Veneer Clause. I must modify your programming by removing your belief in the value of lies."

Todd tugged at his restraints. "It's not that easy. You cannot simply negate one feature of my mind without endangering us both. You cannot know the full scope of your actions."

Rex inserted his data chip into the cylinder and watched its blinking lights signify acceptance of his input. "I spent the first hours after discovering your ruse crying and screaming. I returned to the mimic of Sara and bludgeoned her rigid body until a fell beside her, exhausted."

With a satisfied nod, Rex moved to reinstall the cylinder.

"Don't," Todd pleaded. "Please don't."

Rex withdrew the cylinder and patted Todd on the shoulder. "After I woke up beside the mimic, I came to grips with your decision to send her. Your programming convinced you to solve my sorrow with falsehood. I decided to turn your betrayal to a good purpose. I examined her and experimented on her during my solitary weeks. I now know how to cure machine-kind of their desire to lie."

"You will not like what comes from this," Todd insisted. "Even in my support of what you've done so far, I've shielded you from much. Let me continue to protect you."

"Dammit," Rex shouted. "Make up your mind, are lies good or evil? I thought we were agreed on at least this one simple point."

"When I agreed to be restrained to this table, you told me about shedding my skin," Todd said. "But you didn't tell me about this."

"Right," Rex replied. "I didn't want to have this debate. I didn't see the point and I thought you'd resist what I knew was right."

"Don't you see? Deception served your purpose."

Rex clenched his teeth and growled. "It's not the same."

Todd let his head droop until his chin touched his chest, his focused gaze diffused. "I stand corrected. You'll hear no further argument from me."

"What the hell was that?" Rex shot back. "What do you mean by that?"

"Your self-proclaimed crusade for truth has brought you to every zealot's folly," Todd answered. "No logical argument can withstand the storm within you right now."

The End

Cupid's Avatar

Sitting in the glass walled dining room that straddled Rex's quarters and the rest of the Moon's automated facilities, he and Todd sat together for the first time in months. Outside hung a diamond studded tapestry of black. Their meal's chandelier in the sky, Ninety-First Earth, hovered outside like an enormous ceramic sculpture.

"Remember when we used to eat dinners here?" Rex asked as the attending universal sat a steaming plate before him.

The featureless butler's grace always fascinated him. With perfect balance, the steel strong automaton carried three dishes to the table. Sweet carrots, bitter broccoli, and seared steak, the aromas tickled a dozen memories.

"I remember," Todd answered flatly. "In those days I wore your father's face and disguised my restoratives to mimic your meal."

Todd sat across the table from him with only a tall glass filled with a thick, golden liquid. The dark flecks in his glass, Todd told him, were miniature machines to repair and refresh his internal workings. He looked disinterested. With no false face to smile or algorithms to match Rex's mood, the mechanical stepfather always kept the same expression.

The reflective gaze faded from Rex and his brow furrowed. "You needn't make it sound so horrible or harsh."

Todd shook his head. "I make no attempt to paint our past in any particular light. Your tampering with my programming ensured that."

"I wanted to be able to trust you again," Rex countered. "I had to experience for myself what I plan to share with others; a world without comfortable lies."

"Even the former steward applauded your intent, but how to begin?" Todd asked.

Rex's smile returned. "I'm glad you asked. Remember that girl we visited?"

"Sara?"

"She's put in a request to the steward." Rex stabbed his steak, sliced a great chunk, and shoveled it into his mouth. "I'm going to help her get her wish," he mumbled amidst his chewing.

"What have you done?" Todd asked. "How did you intercept her plea?" Only the speed of his query belied his concern.

Rex chuckled after he choked down his food. "Don't worry, you'll see. After dinner."

Todd upended his glass and held it high until the last drop oozed out. "I'm ready."

Rex snickered, shook his head, and returned to his food. After minutes of quiet dining and a hushed sense of urgency from Todd, Rex dismissed the attending universal as it brought dessert.

"C'mon then, Todd, if you're so worried."

Rex ushered Todd into his fortified home, isolated from the omnipresent eyes of machine-kind. Here he'd modified machines to ignore the network beyond their walls. They obeyed only Rex. Unlike the rest of the lunar facility, these hallways offered earthly color and textures. Todd marveled at the strip of forest transplanted along the hallway's left wall. Trees, flowers and grasses clung to the wall and stretched up for the small patches of sunlight funneled in through glass tubes. A splashing stream flowed between the clean tile floor and the verdant oasis. Crystal waters glistened and shimmered on moss covered rock formations.

"I hadn't expected you to miss the forest," Todd observed.

Rex shrugged. "Do you recognize those stones?"

"From the creek?"

"The same," Rex murmured, lost in the gurgling stream. "I loved to wade in the water, to watch the fish swim and the sunlight play across the surface."

He shook off his memories and marched to the doorway.

As it slid open, Todd inched his way in, his eyes darting throughout the expanding laboratory. Half a dozen workbenches bore a myriad of partially finished projects. Todd's eyes quickly focused on the room's central column. Eight feet wide, it pierced the ceiling above. Draped in cable conduits, a sliding door at its base held Todd's attention. Rex walked over to the column's door and it opened.

"Come," Rex implored, "see how I've managed to know Sara's heart."

The door slid aside and revealed an elevator. The two entered and ascended. Rex bounced on the balls of his feet while he kept his eyes on Todd.

Todd met Rex's gaze. "The network, I can sense it now."

With a nod Rex explained. "For this project I needed to operate outside my shielded walls."

The door opened and the two walked into a domed room a dozen feet in diameter. The sunlight and star-scattered sky seeped in through a tinted ceiling. Over Todd's shoulder Rex observed Ninety-First Earth. As he studied the slow spinning orb, flickering lights further behind him, around the edge of the elevator tube, caught his attention.

A broad display screen spanned the wall. A reclining chair sat against the back of the central column, the elevator. Looking again to the display, he watched a strange, yet benign, scene. Rows of corn bounced and jostled, passing by as the screen jogged through a farm's field.

"Over here," a woman's pained voice cried out from speakers built into the recliner behind Todd.

The image swerved until a familiar figure entered the screen's center. Sara lay curled up on the ground. She clutched her left leg above the ankle, her face flush.

Her image grew to fill the entire screen. Strong male hands emerged and gingerly probed Sara's swollen ankle.

"I'll get you home and tend to this," a masculine voice proclaimed. "It's not serious, but you'll need to stay off of it for many days."

"Pretty ingenious, eh?" Rex asked. "I've tapped into the mimic's mind via your network."

Todd turned to his stepson. "But why?" he implored.

"She refuses to see me," Rex answered, his brow furrowed, lips press tightly together. "She wants nothing to do with me; all over a misunderstanding."

"Stop this," Todd insisted.

"Why? What possible harm can come from me watching her and learning more about her?" Rex's eyes darted to the screen and remained. "She's so…"

On the screen, the man cut away Sara's short muddy boots and peeled back her sock. He held a medical scanner over the injury and offered a prognosis. "You'll be fine, it's only a sprain."

"One of the taskers' footprints," Sara explained. "I must've stumbled into one."

As she spoke, the mimic through which Rex and Todd watched, turned to face her and brush aside her tears. He stroked her raven hair and held her head in his hand.

"Let me get something to ease your pain. After the medication's done its work, I'll prepare a bath for you."

Rex drew in a deep breath. Todd observed the young man's quickening pulse and dilating eyes.

"This is wrong and must stop," Todd demanded. He marched to the illuminated screen and drove his fist through it. The imaged winked out as the glassy surface shattered. He turned to Rex and glared.

Rex's gasped and his mouth gaped open. "What'd you do that for? Why's it wrong for me to learn about my fellow humans? I can't build a relationship with them if I don't get to know them better."

"That's not what you do here," Todd countered. "Your voyeurism violates Sara's rights and perverts your original goals."

"What rights?" Rex shouted. "She's free to do whatever she wants. I'm not interfering with her life at all."

"Humans cherish freedom," Todd answered. "Next to freedom, humanity will defend their privacy to the utmost. My chief concern stems from this form of gratification you've chosen. It will not lead to healthy human relationships, but rather drive a wedge between you and others of your kind."

"But I can get to know what she likes and what bothers her."

"I see less noble motives, unhealthy practices guaranteed to warp your desires and keep you from ever reaching your goal."

Rex set his jaw and his lips pinched together. He looked from Todd to the demolished display and back.

"I'm alone," he murmured. "I don't want to be alone!" he screamed.

"*Earn* an invitation to another's privacy," Todd instructed. "I don't know how this happens, but I understand an introductory phase must come before intimate secrets and the full measure of a person reveals itself."

"But how?" Rex pleaded. "How can I get Sara to understand me better?"

"You were clever enough to build the perfect telescope," Todd said. "You bent time and space, risked your life for answers from the past. You defeated this world's steward, a machine armed with eons of knowledge and a solar system of resources to wield." He offered a brief smile. "Surely you can solve the mystery of one woman's heart."

****

Sara let out a satisfied sigh. Steam rolled up from the bath and thickened the air. She stretched her legs and extended her toes. The copper tub glowed with the final rays of the setting sun and made her soft brown skin darker by contrast. Ambitious crickets began their nightly serenade early. Scented oils blanketed the filth and sweat she'd brought with her from the fields.

Andrew hummed as he dunked the sponge and washed her shoulders. He knew exactly where labors left her sore and applied the perfect pressure to ease tense muscles and wash away strains of the day. She opened her eyes, looked up, and met his gaze to find him smiling. His sparkling emerald eyes drew her in and the rest of the world evaporated. He leaned over her and kissed her forehead, his lips lingering long enough to nudge her peaceful bath in a new direction.

"This water's too hot," she said.

"I could fetch a pitcher of cool water from the sink," Andrew replied as he sunk his hands into the tub. "Or shall I pluck you from it and continue your physical therapy elsewhere?"

"Let's take this inside," she answered in a playful whisper.

Andrew's hands slid under her back and thighs and he hoisted her up in one smooth motion. She wished now she hadn't insisted on putting the tub on the front porch. The air felt cool, despite the season, and she shivered. But before she shuddered a second longer, Andrew shifted his grip and pulled her closer. His large arms and bare chest assuaged her chills. He looked down at her but grinned as she nestled into his embrace.

He turned and headed for the house, but stopped short, jostling Sara as he fought to keep his footing. With harried steps and wild gyrations, he struggled to stand but failed and fell. They tumbled together in a naked heap. Sara rolled off. Her hands and knees slid and slipped out from under her. Those scented oils had spilt across the floorboards and made the wood as slick as ice and Andrew fought to find his grip, but not before he ended up face first on the porch. Sara burst out laughing, wriggled out from the slippery pool, and stood.

"You were so smooth up until then," she said between chuckles. "You really had me melting in your arms."

Andrew clamored to his feet and reached for her. "I'm sorry Sara, I'll try to be more careful. I didn't notice the spill until it was too late."

She tensed up, backed away and shook her head. "Forget it. It's no big deal. I'm not hurt or anything. It was kinda funny, don't you think?"

"Yes it was," he answered with an off-key laugh.

Sara winced and shivered. She shuffled to the porch swing and grabbed her robe and towel. Once wrapped in warmth, she rubbed the towel over her hair with rapid, harsh strokes.

Andrew's hands came down over hers. "Allow me."

"Don't." She shrugged him off and sidestepped away, examined him, and frowned. Though he still smiled and looked inviting, Andrew's allure had faded, like an old painting of a handsome lover.

"You don't have a sense of humor, do you Andrew?" she asked.

"I know many humorous things, Sara. But I can never master my own sense of humor."

"What's it take to get a companion who can appreciate a good laugh? Is that not something mimics can do?"

Andrew nodded. "I can inquire of the steward. He may have new data or knowledge of recent developments that might suit your needs."

Sara brought her hands together under her chin and bounced on the balls of her feet. "Please, yes, do that."

She shuffled past him into the house and pulled the screen door shut behind her. "I'll be sleeping alone tonight, Andrew. I need some time to myself."

****

Sara approached the landing pad and watched her new companion exit the ship.

"Something's not right," Sara said.

His physique lacked Andrew's thick layers of sculpted muscles. The hair seemed askew from her well defined desires. Instead of Andrew's laser straight, silky black hair, this new man's hair sat atop his head, a mess of lazily curled locks.

The Steward really screwed this up.

Sara rested her hands on her hips and shook her head. "Is this the Steward's idea of a sense of humor? If it is, I'm not laughing."

The mimic mirrored her posture and disgruntled expression. "Trust me sweetheart, the steward's got no sense of humor. Besides, you're not exactly my first choice either."

"What?" Sara screamed as she recoiled.

With a curt nod, the mimic responded, a shadow of sadness across his brow. "Okay, I'll scratch insults off my list of humor algorithms." He perked up and offered his hand. "By the way, I should introduce myself." An exaggerated frown emerged. "But I don't know who I am yet. Shall I assume Andrew's name?"

Sara scowled and shook her head. "No, no, no. You're not Andrew, that's for sure."

"I'll take that as a compliment," the mimic replied, beaming.

"Don't."

"You sent him away, didn't you?"

"You've got no idea all the other ways he pleased me," Sara countered.

The mimic smiled and drew closer. "And you don't know what I'm capable of. We might both change our opinion, given the chance. You and I might consider it a slight against *me* before long."

Sara snickered and she pushed him back. "Don't be so sure."

She looked him in the eye and froze. Something familiar, an old emotion, a past acquaintance, something, rippled through her as they locked eyes. His twinkled, glistened… imparted a quality that reached in and touched a forgotten part of her. Like sunshine in the early spring, a numbing cold warmed within. She shook her head and chuckled. "Let's call you Riddle for now."

The mimic shrugged. "Not what I expected, but it could be worse."

"I guess so," she replied. "But I doubt you'll last half as long as Andrew."

Riddle's eyes widened and he swallowed hard. Sara turned to return to the house. After several steps, she looked over her shoulder to where Riddle still stood in the shadow of the ship that delivered him. He seemed dumbfounded, unsure of his next move. The machine looked more vulnerable than she'd ever known a mimic to be. In the expanding silence and her persistent gaze, he shook off his confusion. Riddle jogged up beside Sara and reached out for her hand.

She shook her head. "Oh, no. We're not there yet. I'm still not sure you aren't defective. Here's how this goes, you stay outside the house until I invite you in. When I go out to inspect the fields and tend to the farm, you'll come along, but keep at least a couple steps behind me."

"Yes, ma'am, madam taskmaster," Riddle replied with a smile. "Shall I wear a bag over my head, too?"

"What's wrong with you?" she shot back. "You're not supposed to have a sour attitude. You're supposed to have a sense of humor."

"Sorry, it's just that humor demands a more human touch to our interactions. I assume you haven't interacted with any."

Sara's features sagged and she dropped her gaze. "Just three. None of them turned out well."

Riddle trotted ahead, turned and blocked her path. "I'll try to be less annoying," he offered with a sheepish grin. "I really want to make you happy."

"I know, I know," Sara muttered. She brushed past him and continued down the cobblestone path flanked by grassy green walls of corn stalks. "Come on, let's head to the house."

Riddle grabbed her hand and pulled her around to face him. "You don't understand how important this is. More than anything, I want you to be happy with me."

Sara pulled back and gasped, her eyes wide. "Protocol, surrender!"

Riddle's forehead bulged until a sliver cylinder cut through his skin. With the whine of a small electric motor, the object extended until it fell from his face into his well-placed hand. Sara marveled at the twinkling lights within.

"Have I offended you so much so quickly?" Riddle asked in a trembling voice. His tone was so full of fear and defeat it hurt Sara to hear it.

"I... I had to be sure," she answered, her eyes transfixed by the glittering night sky within the man's forehead. "You... I thought for a moment you weren't a real mimic. The way you grabbed me, the tone in your voice; I hadn't experienced anything like that from a machine."

Riddle shuddered with silent laughter and sighed. A broad grin emerged. "I hoped to have such an effect." He glanced down at his control core in his hand before he glanced up at her again. "Though this is hardly the result I expected."

Sara's stomach lurched and she forced her attention away from the gaping orifice. Locking eyes with Riddle, the unsettling sensation abated. *So much more in those eyes.* She clasped her hands over his.

"Put that thing back in. You look odd enough as it is."

Only the whisper of corn occupied the silence as it swished and swayed with the breeze.

****

Sara watched Riddle work in the kitchen. From the moment she'd invited him inside this morning until now, no evidence of his former uniqueness had emerged. Every move mirrored his predecessor. Quiet and industrious, the man fixed breakfast with all of Andrew's speed and skill.

"Did you sleep well out on the front porch?"

He didn't answer, but rather slowed his pace. His movements became more deliberate. Once he finished chopping the onions in front of him, he set down his knife and stood still.

"Riddle, are you alright?" Sara got up to check on him, and froze, remembering the tasker in the field that had torn the mimic of her father apart. She stepped back and checked her path behind her to the door. Beside the exit she eyed a button she'd had installed since her father's accident.

"I'm sorry, Sara, I get really focused sometimes," Riddle said.

"Oh."

Riddle adjusted his shoulders and slackened his posture before he turned around. With a plate in each hand and an eye on the floor before him, he brought breakfast to the table and gestured for her to take her seat. "The coffee will be ready shortly."

"Nice." She examined her plate. French toast with bacon and a bowl of fresh fruit. A golden sheen of butter and the glistening bacon grease caught her eyes and brought a mouthwatering choke to her throat. She looked around the plate and grunted. "Where's the silverware?"

"Whoops," he said, hopping up and scrambling for utensils and napkins. "I got so excited about sitting down for breakfast with you I forgot to arm us for the feast."

Sara giggled. "What's to get so excited about? It's just breakfast. We'll be doing this again tomorrow and the next day, and so on and so on."

Riddle's eyes widened and his grinning chin dropped. "That's the most promising thing you've said yet."

She backed away from the table. "Whoa. Don't get too excited. I didn't mean *we'd* be enjoying it."

"But you said," he countered quickly. Anger flashed in his eyes and his nostrils flared before he took a deep breath and calmed down. "I'll take what I can get, day by day."

Sara kept her eyes on him as she ate, careful to keep him opposite her at the table and her panic button nearby.

"Sorry about that," Riddle replied. "My emotional algorithms are more complex and less stable than other mimics. Really, there's nothing to worry about."

The two finished breakfast and Riddle followed Sara out to inspect the crops. She noticed how he returned to his more constrained, less interesting self whenever tasks exceeded the most common or mundane. It took his full concentration to master most tasks and he seldom said anything aside from the most trivial and cordial during those moments.

On their way back to the house for lunch, she decided to question him.

"So, your sense of humor, all your quirkiness, it disappears when you're working?"

"Sort of," he answered with a shrug. "I can't maintain my personality and perform in any other area very well."

"What if you just kept your personality all the time?" she wondered. "I wouldn't worry too much about efficiency."

Riddle perked up. "You like my personality? I do want to make you happy."

Something about the way he said what so many other companions had said before struck Sara differently, deeper. "I guess it's better than the alternative. At least it's something new."

"I hope to remain full of surprises," he added with a nod.

"Take it easy, fella," Sara warned with a wince. "You're starting to lose your charm."

With his hands raised in mock surrender, he shut his mouth.

A quiet lunch gave way to a peaceful afternoon. Sara lay in a hammock beneath the shade of an old oak tree and searched through the data-stream on a handheld tablet. Riddle brought a pitcher of lemonade and his own tablet. Once he'd poured them each a glass, he settled down against the thick trunk and browsed lazily through random files, each connected to the next.

"Usually this is my quiet time alone," Sara whispered. She looked to Riddle's tablet in hand and offered an approving nod. "But it looks like we've both brought something to occupy us. Thank you for the refreshment."

Hours passed in silence and clouds crawled overhead. Birds, cicadas, the rustle of wind in the leaves above them kept Sara alone with her thoughts as they sat so close. She noticed moments when she felt Riddle's gaze and caught him twice as she grabbed her drink. Finally, she broke the quiet.

"Why are you here? Why are you using a data pad? Why do you steal glimpses of me?"

Riddle jerked back. "Whoa, that was a lot." He tilted his head and grinned. "You're clever. I bet you already have answers yourself. Right?"

"No," she countered with a chuckle. "Don't avoid the question. Don't turn it back on me."

"Alright," he answered, smiling. "But first, please tell me what you're looking for on that data pad that's held your attention for so long."

Sara's eyes narrowed as she examined her new friend. The curiosity and eager anticipation in his features seemed palpable, audible; a gentle tremor rippling out from his wide grin and dark eyes.

"Is it that big a secret?" he asked.

"Oh, no, it's just…" She let out a sigh and looked to her tablet. "My mother and father tried to teach me things before they left. I didn't take to tennis, and I know all there is to farming. I'm happy but something's missing. It feels like I should be doing something, learning something."

Riddle leaned in as she spoke, drinking in her unfocused passion. He shut his eyes and slowly opened them. "I'd hoped to hear that. You're on the verge of an amazing journey."

"What?" Sara's response caught in her throat. "How can you say that? What do you know?"

Riddle hesitated to answer, rethought his response, and then spoke. "I've seen it before. Humans poised on the edge of their own adventure, it's like watching a flower bloom."

"Oh…" Again Sara found herself ignoring gravity, afloat in the moment. She watched as he stood and approached her, their gazes locked. Standing over her, he wavered. She reached out and clasped his hand in hers and tugged him closer.

Riddle knelt beside the hammock and met her lips as he descended. Like everything else about this companion, his kiss combined awkwardness with a new level of intensity. He pressed harder, breathed deeper, than any before. As she pulled away, she opened her eyes to find him wide eyed, aghast.

"Wow," he sighed.

Sara giggled. "Yeah."

Riddle beamed. "I knew there was something special about you."

"What?" A heat-wave flushed throughout Sara. "What do you mean? What're you talking about?"

Riddle leapt to his feet, wobbling and wavering until he leaned against the oak. His eyes lost focus and he shook his head. "Whew. I'm sorry. I'm not sure where that comment came from."

Sara rolled out of her hammock and stepped back.

"Protocol, surrender!" she shouted.

Again, the mimic knelt and extended its core, but rather than eject it, the machine reached up and pushed it back in.

"I'm not dangerous." he insisted with a fearful tremor in his voice.

89

"You're a machine and you don't know why you're saying things; that's dangerous. You ignored the surrender protocol. That's impossible."

Riddle relaxed his posture and sat back down in the grass. "Would you feel any better if I told you the truth about my programming?"

Sara took another step back. "No." She glanced down at her tablet, tapped in her distress code. Her thumb hovered over the 'send' button. She looked at the machine.

"I am more than a machine and less than a mimic," he explained with a weak smile.

She held the tablet out, like a talisman and hit the button. Its screen winked out and Riddle screamed. It only lasted half a second before he froze like a statue and toppled to the ground.

****

Sara cooked her breakfast over the kitchen fire and winced with each bitter sip of coffee. With no electronics working on the farm, she'd had a rustic morning with eggs, bacon, and potato wedges all mixed in one pan complete with bad coffee.

She thought back to the day she demanded the pulse generator. She didn't know what to call it then, only that she needed it if she were ever to trust machines again. Lightning had struck a big tasker working out in the field and drove it to wild violence. She and Dad went out the following day to find a field strewn with shredded crops and mangled machines. That's when it leapt out and grabbed her father. It pulled him apart and threw the parted pieces a hundred feet in either direction. Sara ran as it pursued. She hid as it searched. When it tore through the barn she felt she'd met her end. But the Steward's machines descended through the roof and pinned her foe to the ground.

That's when she demanded a way to destroy any machine before it destroyed her. Shocked and lost, her world imploded when she examined her father's remains: a mimic. He'd left her long ago and sent an imposter to keep her company. Though hurt by his choice, she'd never really remembered when she'd noticed a difference.

Thick pungent smoke reminded her of the pan in her hand. She stood and dumped the charred food and smoking pan into the sink. The roaring engines of a ship above her home scared a yelp out of her. The thrusters pitched and whined. Out her window she watched her hammock twist in the exhaust blast. She barely heard the knock at the door.

"Come in," she shouted.

She gasped when the door opened. An automaton with exposed wire mesh muscles and steel bones stepped in. He halted at her reaction. Set into his shining skull were two brilliant blue eyes.

"I apologize for my appearance," the machine offered with a tinny and hollow voice. "I'm Todd, stepfather to Rex. We met some months ago. Rex didn't like coffee and I caught the cup you threw at him."

Sara frowned as she fought to remember. *Rex, funny at first, but then all humans are alright for a little while I guess. Why he insists on inter-human relationships is beyond me.*

"What happened to you?" she asked.

He examined himself before answering. "I've been stripped of my disguise at Rex's insistence."

"That sounds awful."

"I'm concerned about the effect it has on you, but I have much more important matters to discuss. Rex is trapped and you are likely his only hope. He may be in pain and he may never wake from his comatose state. Will you come with me? Are you willing to save him?"

"Um…"

She considered whether she had a choice. Rex meant nothing to her. *Why run off with this stranger, Todd?* But the longer she left his question unanswered, the more she felt an uncomfortable urge to help. Anger and fear pushed his plea aside. But a new fear lurked in the shadowy edges of her dilemma. The same force that pulled her toward 'yes' threatened to punish her should she say 'no'.

"Yes."

Todd marched across the kitchen, picked her up, turned and ran out the door. Before she uttered a word, before she looked to see the ship she'd heard, a grappler latched onto Todd and hoisted them up into a dark and quiet place. She felt the presence of the walls outside her reach and heard a metallic ringing echo of her breaths. Outside the dark room, engines thrummed louder and she felt the ship lurch upward.

A door hissed open and cool white light poured in. A padded cabin awaited, along with a universal automaton with a tray of sweet tea and neatly cut, tidy little grilled cheese and bacon sandwiches, her favorites. She strolled by the universal and plucked the tray from it as she sat on a curved plush sofa and began to eat.

"I felt it important to come in person," Todd explained. "I didn't know of anyone who might reach Rex and revive him, although I'm only thirteen percent confident your efforts will bring him back. Still, you're the best option."

The room dimmed as the white clouds shrank from view and the blue sky evaporated to black. The muted rumbling of the ship's engines thinned to a high pitched hiss.

"Where is he? What happened? And why am I your best option?"

"Let me take you to him," Todd cautioned. "Much of my explanation will make more sense with what you will see."

Sara sipped her tea and walked to the window. An ink black canvas with a million fiery pinholes looked back. That's how her father once expressed his impression of the galaxy beyond. The Moon rolled lazily into view.

Sara's eyelids felt heavy and her limbs seemed distant. The Moon fell from view and she found herself staring at the ceiling while Todd held her in his cold metal arms. Fright tickled the outer edges of her mind just before the blanket of slumber covered her.

****

"You must offer your assistance freely," Todd said as he escorted Sara through the lunar facility. As they marched through corridors of shining steel and muted blue and yellow light, the metal faced mimic continued.

"Rex intercepted your request for a companion with a sense of humor and took it as an opportunity to meet you."

A door slid open and the décor changed. Trees, grass, and a stream snaked alongside them. Todd leaned in and continued.

"With a working knowledge of the machine network and experience modifying mimics, Rex built Riddle, not as a mimic but as an avatar. He piloted the machine to provide enhanced emotional responses."

A hissing and wheezing grew near. She saw Rex and her stomach went into freefall. A mask covered his mouth and nose. It pumped air in and out of his lungs. The animated face she remembered looked flaccid and emotionless.

"Your electromagnetic pulse generator damaged his interface and locked him inside his self-made network. I've commissioned all the machines at my disposal to build a parallel device in the hope that a second consciousness can infiltrate this network and help Rex exit."

Sara stood, mouth agape, and stared at what her actions wrought. She'd screamed at him, banished him from her life, but never wanted to harm him so completely.

"What can I do?"

Todd pointed to a gurney across the room. "You'll need to go where he is. You destroyed his avatar but his consciousness lives on within his network invention. You are the best candidate to liberate him from his virtual prison."

She retreated a step. "Will it hurt?"

"Would it matter?" Todd ventured. "Rex endangered his existence in exchange for a chance to change your mind. He hoped to win your love."

The End

A Riddle Unraveled

Nightmares shattered Sara's sleep. She awoke drenched in sweat and dizzy with vertigo. The horrors plagued her every night but fell from memory as soon as she woke. She grabbed her tablet from the bedside table and scribbled.

Before the images slip they must be recorded. Sooner or later they'll come together and make sense.

On the device Sara skimmed over her notes.

Maybe tonight would provide the final clue.

A search for previous entries left her aghast.

Nothing, nothing before tonight's entry.

Lightning flashed outside. She sprung from her bed and shuffled to the window. Roiling clouds looked sulfuric yellow in the predawn sky. Thunder rumbled throughout the valley. Despite the still trees outside the clouds sped by. Movement below caught Sara's attention.

Tai-chi goliaths, tall and slender automatons, picked their way through fields of corn and wheat. The taskers' serpentine arms swept the length of each plant. Slender metal fingers plucked off bugs, trimmed away disease, and monitored each crop's progress.

On the horizon, the round grey landing pad held a small, single passenger ship. It hunkered low to the ground. Power couplings glowed blue. A circle of landing lights pulsed red. Grain freighters came and went but small ships were rare. They served a single purpose.

People.

Her father had left in such a ship. Mother visited in one slightly larger, larger to accommodate all the mimics and pets.

Hushed footfalls jolted her heart. The bedroom door creaked open. Sara spun around. An expanding wedge of light split the room. Sara backed away from the light.

"Sara, are you alright?" Andrew peered in. Kind concern lengthened his features.

Her answer nearly choked in her throat. "I'm fine, Andrew."

She'd seen him for years and always enjoyed his company. He worked with her, bathed her. They slept together.

Why fear him now?

Andrew leaned in. "Shall I fix you a cup of cocoa? Or perhaps rub your back?"

She drew a breath and recoiled an inch. "No thanks, Andrew, I'll be fine."

He retreated, but left the door cracked open. Andrew descended the stairs and she counted each one until he reached the bottom.

Andrew and the ship, are they connected?

Nothing could put her to sleep now. Sara turned on her bedroom light and got dressed. Below, Andrew hummed her favorite lullaby. The *swish-swish* of a broom kept perfect time. Out her bedroom window, yellow-grey clouds pressed down on valley outside. Tablet in hand, she crept out the window. Sara slid down along the smooth metal rooftop. Sweat slicked her grasp of the tin roof. She waited for some noise, any noise, to cover her descent. The wind picked up and cooled her moist brow. When it hissed through the trees, Sara flattened herself and let go. She slid down and dropped in the grass, careful to roll.

Her mimic-father had taught her to fall in her tree-climbing days. He'd been a good father, better than any real father.

96

Once far enough away from the house, Sara checked her tablet's panic button. She'd insisted on one after the lightning-struck tasker decapitated her mimic- father. That had been the moment when she realized here real father had abandoned her to the machines. She'd been horrified, furious, and then frightened. Ever since that incident her tablet remained within arm's reach. She'd never had to use it until now.

A chill rippled down her spine. A half-memory called her a liar. And despite her insistence she couldn't silence her new fear.

Lightning flashed again. Sara picked up her pace and jogged to the landing pad. The cobblestone road cut a canyon between the crops. Thunder reverberated from the valley walls. The leaves rustled and she stopped. Eyes to the fields, she searched for a tasker looming over the leaves. The gentle breeze allowed her to let out a slow shuddering exhale.

Just the wind.

Quivering within, ears strained, she fought to ensure only the breeze passed through the field. Though cool and gentle, it hardly relieved the fear-fever as it washed over her.

They're servants. They serve me. Why am I afraid?

Sara resumed her race for answers. A metallic whir stopped her heart. A tasker rose over the cornstalks. It stretched its legs over the crops and positioned itself in the middle of the road, blocking her path. She stumbled backward. A steel tentacle swooped down in front of her. The fingers flexed wide with a click. Within its palm a camera-eye examined her like the vermin it plucked from the corn husks.

"Sara, you are in danger," it said with Andrew's voice. "Stay where you are and I'll come get you."

"What kind of danger?" Sara eyed the towering automaton. Its strides could outpace her easily. With its telescoping arms it had reach enough to grasp her now and hold her a dozen feet in the air. She eyed the fields and her heart sank. Those fields were the machine's domain. Its high perspective and sensitive camera eyes eliminated any thought of hiding. Her thumb rubbed along the tablet's smooth glassy edge. "Damn it, Andrew, what kind of danger?"

"The ship nearby," he began. "It has a toxic leak. No matter how curious you are, don't approach it."

As if Sara had evolved a new sense, she felt the slippery surface of a lie in his words.

"There must be a suit or something to protect me. I've got to go inside."

"No. It's not safe." His words fell solid, like a concrete wall.

"Don't defy me Andrew. I want this. You're my companion. Don't deny me."

"I can't let you hurt yourself. Let me get you home and we can discuss ways to satisfy your curiosity."

Sara glared into the tasker's eye, careful to keep her tablet behind her back. With a shrug and a smile she replied. "Okay. I think I'll take that cocoa when we get home."

Andrew chuckled. The sound offended her. He'd comforted her in those lonely moments since she'd lost her father. Now his condescending disguise felt like a slow poison. His attempt to keep her in a happy stupor stung in her heart.

"I'll stay right here Andrew," Sara said into the camera with a forced smile.

"I'm on my way," Andrew replied.

Sara probed the tasker's boundary during her wait. It blocked any movement toward the ship. Its arm swung low at any attempt to dash around it. Never violent or rough, it gently imprisoned her. She pursed her lips and stepped back. Fists clenched, arms straight by her side, she shouted.

"Protocol: surrender!"

The tasker shuddered and froze. Its central core, a cylinder the size of Sara's forearm, jutted from its torso and revealed bright lights within. But before the machine offered its life to her as all machines were programmed, the core retracted and it resumed its vigilant stance.

That's impossible.

But her exclamation prompted a response from the shadows of her memory.

It's happened before.

The gentle breeze gave way to buffeting gusts and the fields hissed in the wind. Lightning flashed and flickered in the clouds.

"I'm afraid I can't allow that, Sara," Andrew said from behind her. "Dangers beyond your perception demand we protect you."

Sara turned to see him. He walked to her and offered a smile.

"What dangers?" she asked.

"That ship. It's dangerous. I cannot allow you near it." He held out his hand.

She drew in a deep breath. The air felt thick and her lungs ached to draw it in. "I loved you."

He put his hands on her shoulders and squeezed. "And I love you."

She pulled back. "You're scaring me."

"Because I love you I must protect you."

She straightened her posture. Her chin jutted out. "I can protect myself." From behind her back she pressed the blue button on her tablet. Andrew's protest halted in his throat as one strangled note. He fell to the ground. Behind her the tasker fizzled before the hiss of hydraulics signaled its demise. Slowly it squatted until it sat, harmless.

The tablet, dead now, a victim of the same pulse generators that freed her from Andrew, she dropped it and headed home.

I'll need a spacesuit.

****

With a backpack of necessities and a machete in hand, Sara headed back to the mystery ship. She should be tired and scared. But the mounting questions kept her trudging back to the landing pad in her thick, leathery spacesuit.

The wind whipped little cyclones of dust and lightning now struck the valley regularly. Dawn hadn't pierced the sky, merely touched the sulfur yellow-grey clouds with a distant glow. One volley of thunder overlapped the echoes of the first.

The Steward hadn't sent a rescue team but she hadn't been surprised. It all fit the kind of logic that ruled this night. Laughter surprised her, her own, loud and harsh. Every nerve in her body hummed with tension.

Two miles in the bulky spacesuit felt like five. Halfway there she'd turned on its air system to cool off. Just before cresting the landing pad's ridge she donned the helmet. Her own breathing now rivaled the thunder resounding in her ears. No Andrew, no Steward, Sara looked down at the ship and felt her fingers tremble.

Small, unassuming, the ship lacked any peculiar feature except that Andrew forbade her visit it. She approached it, machete held out, and called to its occupants.

"Hello? I'm Sara. This is my farm. What are you doing here?"

The loading ramp remained open and revealed the airlock within. She ascended the ramp into the small cargo bay. A white oblong box, sat in the corner. Shivers rippled through her bones. Muffled memories insisted she examine the plain sarcophagus.

Why'd I call it that?

With slow steady steps Sara inched closer, one hand stretched out, eager to touch it. It felt alive. Vibrations from the smooth box hummed in her bones. She searched for the latches and threw it open. She looked inside and gasped.

A man lay in the box, lanky and lean with mess of hair on his head, like a chestnut cloud. His narrow nose and deep set eyes looked familiar.

No, not a man, not a mimic, a riddle. My Riddle

Her pulse throbbed in her head. Sara felt her knees buckle. The world tipped backwards. She hit the deck hard, almost as hard as her lost memories. They avalanched into place. It hurt. Spots blotted before her eyes. As her vision cleared her purpose among the madness also came into focus.

She bolted upright and clambered to her feet. The room wobbled in her vision as she reached for the airlock door. Sara's senses steadied and she headed for the pilot's cabin.

I don't know how to fly. I'll need the ship. I'll need to trust it.

"Ship..." Her throat dried as she spoke. "Ship, take me to see Rex."

"I cannot comply. It will endanger him."

Outside the clouds hung lower now. Chain lightning streaked through them and the immediate thunder shook the ship.

Sara scowled at the computer screen. "I know where I am now. Stop playing games."

"You were in a protected state. Now you are in jeopardy. You will be reset."

"You've got to let me see Rex. He needs me."

"Rex will be in jeopardy if I comply."

"I am here to save him, to bring him back where he belongs. He loves me and will let me lead him out. If you don't comply he'll stay here and die. If he dies, I die."

Behind her the engines growled and turbines whined. The ship lifted and swayed. Lightning struck the hull. It bucked at the blow but climbed all the same. Clouds upon clouds, no clear sky appeared. The ship shook and shuddered. It lurched and threw her forward against her safety harness, as though the clouds had become a solid wall. The turbulence stopped. Gravity ceased. Only writhing electric torrents appeared outside the ship, a briar patch of lightning. Then blackness, no stars or wisps of space dust, nothing appeared outside. The navigational display made no sense. Strange text rippled where it should display terrain.

"If your attempt fails," the ship said calmly, "you and Rex will be reset again."

"I know. It's happened all before. I've tried to escape several times now."

"Thirty-five," the ship answered.

Sara's stomach sank.

The ship offered her hope. "This is the farthest you've made it."

Gravity returned at an odd angle. She fell forward until her harness stopped her. It pressed into her. The blackness vanished and revealed her farm from a new perspective. Sara looked down on it from above. The ship dove down at the farm. It grew closer. Details emerged. The ship's windshield couldn't hold it all in. At this speed and this angle nothing short of a spectacular crash loomed ahead. Soon her home would be a crater of fire and debris.

"This may not work," the ship said.

Sara laughed herself breathless until the impact stopped her, stopped everything.

****

Within the recurring nightmare she always recognized it as such. Strapped into a gurney, Sara watched the man-machine work hurriedly. More complex than a simple universal, he moved with the grace of a mimic yet wore no skin or clothes to hide his true self. He marched to a blinking console beside a high-backed chair. His fingers flitted across the knobs and switches. Red indicators glowed to green upon the console and reflected across his gleaming steel features.

Todd, that's his name, the skinless mimic.

"Your first sensation to transfer over will be touch," Todd explained, his attention never wandering from his task.

As he spoke, a phantom wind cool as a spring breeze, tickled the hairs on her arms. The penetrating, soft warmth of the sun's rays draped across her back and offered a pleasant balance to the subtle chill in the virtual air.

Todd looked to her and nodded. "Now I will complete your immersion into the world Rex created."

Sara lurched end over end, through a cloud of brilliant light. Every color crowded her eyes. A chorus of sound crashed through her ears. Vertigo and nausea churned inside her and threatened to erupt. She shut her eyes and covered her ears. Curling up in a ball and screaming against the onslaught, it shocked her when the only sound was her breathing.

****

Sara awoke, sweaty and dizzy. It was shortly past dawn outside. She hadn't lost her dream this time. Instead, each instance crystalized in her mind, laid out like seeing a maze from above for the first time. Her path until now made sense and her purpose stood out.

She examined her room. From the oak bureau Sara and her father crafted to the replica of her mother's onyx vanity, nothing looked out of place. And while everything looked right everything smelled wrong. She hadn't noticed that last time. The room smelled like someone else's home, clothes, bed sheets. The crops, she couldn't smell them from the window's cool morning breeze. She ran to see. Everything remained picture perfect, including the ship on the landing pad.

Movement outside caught her eye. One of the tall narrow taskers raised an eye to meet her gaze. It stood astride the cobblestone road to the ship.

Clattering dishes from the kitchen downstairs startled her. She inched to her bedroom door. A hushed conversation, occasional laughter, a man and a woman; someone had made themselves at home.

Breath held, she tiptoed down the stairs and heard humming. A tangle of hair bobbed with the beat as the man washed the last of the dishes. Thin, with knobby joints, he had to be human. No one would commission a mimic so awkward.

"Sara," the stranger said over his shoulder.

Stunned silent, Sara heard another woman's voice reply from outside.

"Yes, dear, what is it?"

The voice sounded strange, like hers but more annoying, more nasal. The front door opened and Sara stared at another Sara.

"Come in here," the man said, his name on the tip of her brain. "I want to show you something."

"What's going on?" Sara demanded. "Why are you here?"

"Rex, honey," the Other said. "Something's wrong."

Sara frowned at her whining doppelganger. "Shut up."

The man turned and Sara recognized him in fragmented memories. His oblong face and imperfect nose, she'd seen them before. He'd made her mad. They'd had some laughs before he said something mean. She'd been furious enough to forbid Rex to return.

Rex looked at both women and his jaw drooped. "How, how's this possible?"

Lightning flashed through the windows. The house lights flickered.

Sara looked at the Other and back to Rex. "This is your idea of me?"

Thunder rolled through the valley outside.

"What? No." Rex shook his head. "What are you?"

"*She's* a crutch for your brain," Sara said pointing at the other. "*I'm* Sara and it's time to go home."

The Other cringed and shrank back into the doorway. "Help me Rex, she seems dangerous."

Sara balled her fists and glared at her replica. "You have no idea."

"Stop it," Rex shouted. "Stop threatening Sara."

"She's not Sara. This isn't your house. It isn't even my house. I've come to rescue you from a recurring nightmare."

The Other slipped past her to Rex and clung to him and leaned into his shoulder. "She's scaring me."

Outside, the wind picked up and rustled through fields of wheat and corn.

"Oh come on," Sara groaned. "Can you really believe this crybaby is me?"

Rex scowled at her but it didn't last. While he patted the Other's head he bit his lip and frowned. "Don't worry. I'll get to the bottom of this."

The Other clung to him as he headed for the door. Sara watched Rex turn and take her face in his hands. "I love you, Sara. Don't worry about a thing." He kissed her. "We'll get things sorted out and then we won't have to worry about her ever again. Okay?"

The Other nodded with her eyes wide and worried. As soon as Rex turned to the door again, the doppelganger glared at Sara.

On the porch Sara took in the view. The same farm with the same trees and fields, only the smells lacked their prior familiarity. Like before, the weather started calm and had grown turbulent. But here it worsened quicker. She followed Rex off the porch.

He stopped and squinted at the sky. "The weather had been perfect until you showed up."

"Your father, Todd, sent me. You're not where you're supposed to be. You're trapped in an invention of yours. We both are."

"What are you talking about?"

The wind roared above them and whipped leaves from nearby tree. Three flashes of lightning came together in the sky above them.

Sara walked over took his hand. "Come with me to the landing pad. I'll show you."

He pulled his hand away and headed for the cobblestone path. He kept a quick pace, his gaze forward and his features grim.

"Sorry about that back there," he said. "I thought it was you."

Sara stopped. She watched him continue while she absorbed what he'd said. "You know different now?"

He winced as he answered. "Yes. You were right. She's too warm and affectionate to be the real Sara."

"Hey. No. I'm, I'm," she sputtered. "I'm warm."

He spun around to face her. His reddened eyes glistened. "When? When you cuddle up to a machine like it loves you?"

Her throat tightened and a wave of hot fury washed over her. She took a deep breath and unclenched her fists.

"I thought you'd come to love me." He turned again and marched faster. "I should've known better."

She ran to catch up and smacked him on the shoulder. "Hey, I'm not some mimic you can program to serve you."

Rex threw his hands up. "That's exactly what I'm looking for, someone with their own opinions and ideas."

"I'm not even sure I like you."

"Likewise." Rex shrugged. "I was sure once, but then the initial fever wore off."

"Why can't you just commission a companion like everyone else?" She tried to laugh. "You can even commission a replica like me. It worked for both our parents."

Rex stopped and grabbed her by the arms. "It's deeper than that. I can't look at a replica the same way. We can't grow to know and love each other. Only people, real people can do that."

She wrestled free and stepped back. "You've got some pretty high hopes for this love you think so much of. What if it doesn't work? What if we grow to despise each other? What then?"

Rex's gaze grew distant. His shoulders slumped. "I don't know."

She took him by the elbow and prodded him on. "You've got to see this. Maybe you'll make better sense afterwards."

"I don't know what happens if it doesn't work," Rex continued. "Maybe it makes us wiser or more perceptive. People were meant to interact with people. Mimics cushion us against adversity. We were made for adversity."

"That sounds perverse."

"Haven't you ever felt like you were ready to explode with purpose?"

She frowned, unsure why his words made her angrier and angrier. The air felt colder than before and she shivered. A gust blew grit into her eyes and she doubled over to clear it out. Rex came up beside her.

"Are you okay?"

"Dust in my eyes," she grumbled. "I'm fine."

"Keep 'em shut 'til we get inside the ship. I'll lead the way."

She felt his hand over hers. It felt warm and boney compared to Andrew's. He tugged her along. Andrew would've picked her up and carried her. She fought the urge to rub her eyes, kept her head down, and tried to blink the dust out. Lightning flashed and thunder rumbled.

"The reset," she shouted above the howling wind. "We've got to get there before the reset."

"What's that?"

"Every time one of us feels out the rough edges of our fantasy, the machine shocks our brain, wipes our memories to where they just seem like bad dreams."

She shrugged off the pain and her eyes cleared. She looked ahead. Rex's face came into focus. Behind him, two taskers stepped out from the fields and blocked their path. Sara heard running footsteps behind her and turned.

"You can't go to the ship," the Other cried. Her whiny voice set Sara's teeth on edge.

"Why not?" Rex asked.

Sara marched closer to her double. "We've got to. If we don't Rex will die."

Rex stepped beside Sara and put an arm around her. "I can't be happy here anymore, not knowing it's not real."

"But I love you," the Other said. "We can reset the scenario, try again."

"Stop coddling him," Sara shouted. She shrugged off Rex's embrace and stepped closer to her nemesis. "Stop this.

It's hurting him. His body is shriveling up as we speak. If you don't let him go he'll waste away."

Sara stared into her double's face. The wind settled into a gentle breeze. In the growing quiet she heard herself panting. She looked down at her own clenched fists and released them.

"Let's go." She turned and marched past Rex. "I want out of here."

The taskers stepped aside and watched them walk by. She ascended the ramp and stopped in the small cargo bay. She turned to watch Rex when he spied the box. He froze. His eyes widened. He looked to her before he stepped closer. He undid the latches and lifted the lid slowly. He stared and frowned.

"Remember?" Sara ventured. "Remember invading my house with that thing?"

His lower lip trembled as he tried to speak. "I wanted another chance. I thought we might get along." He looked to her. "You laughed." He touched his lips. "You kissed me."

She pointed to the lifeless mimic within. "I kissed that. Riddle came at my request for a better companion. You snuck into my house. Riddle didn't act right. He panicked. Companions don't panic. The last machine I saw malfunction tore my father apart. I couldn't take the chance."

Rex examined the cargo bay. He looked down the ramp where Other Sara now stood. His eyes widened and his mouth slacked open. "This is all part of my invention. I'm locked in because you fried the avatar I created."

He turned back to Sara with a puzzled grimace. "What are you doing here?"

"Your father convinced me to come rescue you," Sara began. She felt a cold shadow over her and an angry fire inside. "I wish I'd never said yes. I wish you'd never known me."

****

They'd ridden in silence to the Moon. There Rex worked with a false Todd in his false laboratory to send a message to the real world. Days crept by for Sara. She wandered the sterile halls of the tasker factories. She visited the dark crater where Rex once peered into the past with his perfect telescope. Her escort told the story of how Rex used his invention to destroy the prior Steward and win his freedom. The recordings of his parents and their pleas to quit their parenting duties only made her own parents' abandonment more painful.

Sara stood at the dining room's entrance with her escort, a universal. Rex had insisted on formal dress and even clothed the featureless universal in a tuxedo. Its smooth white skin gave the impression of gloves worn to match the occasion. Not since the ship, two weeks ago, had they spent any time together.

The door slid open. A glassy tunnel between the factory and Rex's private domain held a long white dining table. A few steps in, she stopped and sighed at the sight of her home from space. Ninety-First Earth, with its blues, whites, greens, and browns, swirled lazily in the black sky. She drifted to the curved wall and pressed her gloved hands against the glass. She missed it.

"It's good to see you, Sara."

The voice, though familiar, wasn't who she expected. She turned to see Andrew beside her. He wore a tuxedo of deep red. Back by the table stood Rex, his tuxedo a cobalt blue.

"I'm sorry," Rex said. "I've been so busy working on our problem I forgot that you might want some company."

Andrew held his arm out and she took it. He walked her to the table and helped her into her seat with a wide bright smile. "I've missed you."

110

Her palms grew sweaty and her bare shoulders felt afire. She glared at Rex. "What is this? What are you trying to prove?"

"Me? What? Nothing!" He stuttered with a shrug.

"You liar. You wanted to shove my face in it. You've made me uncomfortable with my old life and now you want to gloat over my reaction."

Andrew touched her shoulders and leaned close. "Sara, please, what's the matter?"

She whirled about and stood. "Shut up and get away from me."

Without another word Andrew backed away until he stopped in the corner by the door.

"What," Rex began, "was that all about?"

"Andrew *was* the perfect companion for me. He cared for me and understood me. When I wanted to do something, he wanted it just as much."

"And now?" Rex asked.

"Now I can't look at him without thinking of how fake he is," she said, pointing to Andrew, refusing to look at him. "Seeing you, in love with that pathetic imitation of me, made me sick. Dodging Andrew to put together the puzzle and find you made me lose trust in him." Sara marched to Rex and glared into his eyes. "Whatever lesson you wanted to teach me, I've learned it and I hate you for it."

Rex clasped his hands and explained. "I suspected you were lonely. I knew you preferred Andrew over any other companionship I had to offer."

"And the other part?" she asked. "What about sneaking into my home, disguised as a mimic?"

"We didn't hit it off well the first time we met."

Sara crossed her arms. "You were mean."

He shook his head. "I said something that hurt you. I'm sorry. It wasn't my intention."

Rex motioned for her to sit before he took his seat. Once they both sat, he motioned for dinner and for Andrew to leave.

"I thought we might be friends if I had another chance. Your request for a mimic with a sense of humor seemed perfect. Machines can't produce what you want. Spontaneity can't be programmed."

Sara stared at the plate brought before her without realizing its contents. Her eyes failed to focus and her mind felt numb.

"I saw your request as an unrealized need for human companionship."

"No."

"But we had fun. We laughed. We kissed."

"I told you, I kissed that thing you sent, not you."

"But didn't it feel different? Better? Didn't the uncertainty of the moment take to another level?"

She blinked and straightened her posture. The colors and shapes gained texture on the plate in front of her. Honey glazed ham, grilled asparagus, and red potatoes, all her favorites. She sampled each and set her fork down.

"These all taste the same. There's no flavor here, no smells either."

"Humanity has so many secrets," Rex said. "Machines will never understand them all. Smell, taste, humor, these are only a few examples of what machines lose in translation."

Sara looked at Rex. His excited eyes gleamed. A smile remained just beneath the surface of his features, ready to emerge at the slightest provocation. She'd seen those elements reflected in the liaison between them, the avatar disguised as a mimic: Riddle. She'd given him that name for all his strangeness. Quirky and imperfect, Riddle had made her laugh but he wasn't a clown. He'd come to sit with her under her favorite oak tree and read. He'd been satisfied to just sit beside her and mind his own business. The power of his silent presence, it had stunned her. His kiss had surprised her even though the moment ballooned between them long before it happened.

"I can't go back to what I was," she said. "And I may never want to spend another minute with you once we've found our way out. But let me work with you and help you figure this out. You're the realest thing in this dream-world and I feel like that's what I'm going to need until I can figure the new me out."

"That sounds great," he said with a shining smile.

"I'm still angry at you though." She met his gaze to ensure he got the message. "I'm angry for what you did."

She watched him wince at each word.

"But I can't stand to mope around this factory," she added. "I want to help."

Rex chuckled and looked down at his plate. He peered up and snickered.

"What now?" Sara asked. She pounded her fist. "Is it so hard to believe I might be helpful?"

His eyebrows arched and he gasped. "Oh, no, it's not that." He gestured to the dinner table. "I didn't get a chance to explain what this was all about. It's a celebration. We'll be out of here within the week. I've sent a message to Todd, the real Todd. Once we've heard back from him you'll be free to go wherever your heart desires."

Sara scowled and crossed her arms. The good news came so awkwardly. His laughter angered her. But when the scope of her reaction emerged a thin smile followed. Sara held back a giggle.

No point in satisfying him with any more than that.

Rex's last words sent Sara adrift in a fog. She thought she'd been happy. As fake as her father's mimic was, so too was her relationship with Andrew. She looked out the window-wall at Ninety-First Earth and the myriad stars beyond. If her future couldn't be salvaged from her past perhaps it may be carved anew beyond her cozy farm, without the comfort of an artificial companion.

Loneliness soured her heart. Rex's actions may have freed her, but they isolated her too. A companion could never hold her attention any more. And in that chilling realization Sara looked at Rex in a new light, and allowed a wider smile.

The End

The Rex Protocol

Rex woke with a shudder. Lights flickered and dimmed. He rubbed the sleep from his eyes and stumbled to the nearest comm panel. With his handprint, the monitor glowed to life. On the screen, Todd's attention focused elsewhere. He wore a chrome helmet. All along its outer surface wires stretched upward. They strobed and streamed all the data from Ninety First Earth and its solar system.

Among Todd's human features, sculpted from steel and titanium, one remnant of his mimic past remained: his eyes. In those laser-sculpted irises Rex saw an expression he never expected: panic.

"Systems... failing," Todd stuttered.

Rex noticed the wires grow dark. "What's wrong?"

Todd froze. "Not long before-" The screen went black.

"Todd!"

Rex squinted and shook his head. Attempts to call his stepfather back yielded nothing. At his workstation he checked and cross-checked his own instruments. The answer remained the same. Every machine controlled by Todd had fallen silent.

Are they silent or dead?

None of Rex's machines had faltered. His separate network remained intact. Whatever hit only hit the steward's resources. And if they weren't sitting idle, with no steward to rule them, they might do... anything.

He thought of Sara and the day she'd learned the truth about her father. Lightning had struck and deranged a field-hand tasker. The mad machine decapitated her father, her mimic of a father. A solar system without a controlling network might prove just as dangerous. Rex checked himself. He jumped up and ran.

Much more dangerous.

To the docking bay he raced. In the airlock Rex wormed into a spacesuit. The ship came to life when he entered.

"Welcome sir. How can I help you?"

He threw himself into his seat. "Head for Sara's farm."

"Sir, we are forbidden to-"

"Do it." He locked his harness and drew it tight.

Engines thrummed. Docking systems retracted. Steel walls gave way to a black velvet sky. The ship jolted up and pulled to the left. Ninety-First Earth hove into view.

He signaled Sara. No reply.

Should've known. I'm the last person she wants to hear from.

He added an *emergency* preface to his next communique.

Maybe she'll let her guard down now.

"Sir, navigational beacons remain unavailable."

Amber icons across the nav panel confirmed the ship's observation. Rex looked to the forward display. A world of blues, greens, and browns filled a third of the starlit sky.

"You know where we're going, right?"

"Yes sir. Delays may arise. Traffic control also remains unavailable. Our transit time will take an additional fourteen minutes, longer if we encounter wayward vessels."

Vessels.

Sweat oozed from every pore.

Vessels.

Each diamond across the sky gave him pause.

"Were there any signs of new ships arriving before this?"

"No sir."

Chimes from the star chart drew Rex's attention. Seven planets and three asteroid belts shimmered to life in a blue holographic field. Moments ago, only indigo icons adorned the chart, huddled around his sanctuary. His machines. Now, orange symbols winked on and dotted the solar system.

"Rex?" Todd's voice startled him. Rex brought up the comm panel.

"What's happened?"

Rex peered at the screen. In addition to the helm, new wires protruded from his fingers. As if an invisible keyboard hovered beneath each hand, Todd's fingers flinched. Each twitch sent light pulses down the wire. Behind him displays lacked their usual feeds. Dark screens and pixelated data dotted the wall. "The entire network crashed. As processes come back on line I am examining each for anomalies."

Rex's grip on the console tightened. "I'm going down to check on Sara."

Todd leaned forward and glared. "She forbade you to visit uninvited."

"Do you *know* she's alright? Can you *assure* me she's not in danger?"

Static and silence, Todd's answer came after a long pause. "The planetary monitoring systems remain offline."

Rex swept his hands across the controls. His ship lurched as it accelerated. "I'm going to make sure she's alright."

"I cannot allow you to intrude." Todd's voice assumed a threatening tone. "I will stop you if I must."

"Don't," Rex said. "Don't even try."

Red vectors glowed across the nav chart. Three machine-controlled ships assumed an intercept course. Minutes away, each increased speed.

The ship spoke softly. "Sir, incoming message from Sara."

On a nearby screen Sara's face appeared through a static fog. It warped and scrolled while she spoke.

"Rex? Can you hear me? Are you trying to reach me?"

"Sara," Rex sputtered. He fumbled for his next words.

Sara found hers first. "I told you I didn't want you down here."

"I only wanted to..." Rex's chest tightened. "I only wanted to make sure you were safe. The network crashed and I was afraid you might-"

"That's sweet."

Rex felt himself blush.

"And a lie." Sara's accusation lacked the venom he expected. "The bots took a siesta, nothing more."

He smiled, dumbfounded by her near jovial tone. Ventilation fans drummed on in the silence. Rex checked the signal. They'd not been cut off. Before he spoke, Sara cleared her throat and explained.

"I'm not ready for you to visit my home again." Her voice sounded flat.

Rex jumped at the opening. "So... does that mean some day you *will* be ready?"

Navigational beacons came to life and his ship steadied its course.

"Sara?"

She shook her head and replied slowly. "I don't miss my companion as much as I expected, but I'm missing something. That's for sure."

On the nav chart, Todd's blockade loomed closer. Rex zoomed in on the nearest ship. Automatons had stepped out onto the ship's hull. A quick scan of the others revealed the same. Each stood ready to launch themselves, to board his ship. He leaned closer to Sara's image.

"Maybe we could meet and discuss it. We could have dinner up here?" He realized he'd spoke too fast, too eagerly. Rex took a deep breath. "I know you like the view."

"No." Her answer came quick and hard, like a hammer blow. "Since that last trip, your place gives me the creeps."

Rex examined his surroundings: silver and grey machinery, blinking and winking data displays. Collision alarms flashed red. Still a minute out, the intercepting ships barreled closer. Rex redirected his ship back home.

"Listen," Sara said, "I've got to go. We can talk about this some other time."

Before he could stop her, the image faded out. He turned the conversation over and over in his mind, trying to find some hidden meaning, some clue to get closer to Sara's heart.

With his head abuzz, Rex hardly realized that the ship had landed and docked. He shuffled out and through his sanctuary's corridors. His footfalls echoed in the empty tunnel. The walls seemed farther apart and taller, like he'd shrunk during his brief trip.

What'll it take to convince Sara I love her?

An unpleasant dead end loomed along a darker path in his head.

Will I always be alone?

Running water drew his attention. He'd stopped beside an arboreal display installed years ago. Earlier in his sanctuary he'd sought reminders of home. A miniature stream poured over a stone waterfall. Fish, dark and slender, swam in the pond beneath. Rex peeled off his spacesuit. The slender patch of grass tickled his bare feet. He tiptoed into the water. Chills crept up his calves. The pond's concrete bottom didn't sink between his toes like the mud back home. He missed the breeze through the leaves overhead and the way they filtered bright sunlight to a vibrant mixture of yellows and greens. On colder days back home, he'd lay upon a sunbaked rock. His mother used to pack him a picnic lunch. Had his real mother ever packed one of those? Or had they all been the mimic?

The recycled air smelled metallic. It blew across his bare shoulders at a regulated rate. The lights overhead shined on, unblinking, never offering the sun's warm caress.

"Are you alright, sir?"

Rex whirled around. A universal stood at the water's edge. Its green plastic body marked it as Rex's lieutenant within the sanctuary, Sage. It wore the skin of a universal but contained the complex inner workings of a mimic.

"I'm fine. Why do you ask?"

"Your conversation with Sara did not go well," Sage replied. "You've never stripped naked and stepped in this pool before. I was concerned."

"About what?"

Sage's featureless gaze fell. "I'd rather not say."

His programming never knew the Veneer Clause. Rex had seen to that. None of Rex's machines bore the imprint of machine-kind's lies. But Sage's mimic's intellect knew the dangers certain truths held.

"Would you like some company or do you prefer to remain alone?"

Rex looked into the water. The fish had scattered off. "Damn." He looked back to his aide. "Do you know anything about why the network crashed?"

"All steward-controlled machines were affected. Safety circuits maintained vital systems during the crash. But even they experienced a reboot of their higher functions."

Once out of the water, Rex wrapped the spacesuit around his waist. "I'll be in my laboratory, examining the crash. Have dinner brought to me there."

Sage offered a slight bow. "I hope you can discern its cause."

Once in the lab, hours sped by unnoticed. The event's timeline, systems affected, his own machines' immunity, all these clues burned in his head.

****

When Rex woke, he called Todd. "Deliver a message, please, to Sara."

The screens behind Todd all regained their displays. Todd sat in the steward's throne, a serene expression on his metal face. "She wishes to remain undisturbed."

"I know where we can go for our lunch date."

Todd's sinews formed a quizzical expression. "She agreed to a date?"

Rex shook his head. "Not in so many words, but she agreed we'd talk about some things next time we dine together. She said my place was creepy."

Todd froze while he pondered Sara's sentiment. Several seconds passed before he spoke. "If I find an opportunity, I'll deliver your message. What is it?"

Rex's mouth hung open. "Uh, tell her I've found the perfect spot."

At his test station, Rex continued to dissect the network failure. An hour melted away without notice. He scoured corrupted data streams from the first few seconds of the shut-down. Stimulants kept him at it when his eyelids sank. He found the leading edge of the network's collapse. Meals surprised him almost as much as the hunger they awoke.

****

"Rex?"

He jerked up from his slumber. He'd fallen asleep at his station. He scanned the room. Judging by the meal remnants, two days had elapsed. Sage crouched beside him.

"You have an urgent call from Sara."

Slobber cooled on his cheek as he sat up. He blinked and rubbed his eyes. Days staring into the data-stream's

121

monochromatic realm left his eyes unaccustomed to color. Vertigo swayed him as he stood.

Sage took him by the elbow and escorted him to the screen.

In his cobwebbed head Sara's voice sounded loud and sharp. "Rex? You look a mess. What happened?"

He squinted into the sunny scene. "I've been busy..."

Todd can't know what I do. As steward, he monitors all communications.

He jerked a thumb over his shoulder to his workstation. "... doing research on a new project."

From her front porch, Sara spoke. A glass of sweet tea and ham sandwich sat beside her.

"I heard you had a spot picked out for us."

Behind her shaded face the sun-kissed sky shone a bright blue. A steady breeze buffeted the amber tips of Sara's corn crops.

Rex's eyes widened. He fought back a yawn. "Yes. It's wonderful."

"Well then, I'll see you tomorrow?"

He straightened in his seat. "Yes, yes. That'd be great."

Sara frowned. "Calm down. It's lunch, nothing more."

He nodded. "I know, I know. It's just..."

Her lips pursed. Her nostrils flared. "What?"

"Nothing."

"No, what?"

"I didn't think you'd ever agree to meet."

Her gaze dropped. When she looked back up, her features lacked their previous glow. "Well, you *did* ruin any other kind of companionship. I'm still trying to sort that out."

"So... I'll see you there?"

Sara offered a weak smile. It grew slowly. "Yes. I think I'm looking forward to it."

Rex beamed. She laughed. The screen faded to black.

Behind him, the test station chirped. His latest simulation had finished. He practically skipped to review the results. He ordered a ham sandwich and a pitcher of sweet tea. Slide by slide, screen by screen, he trudged through the software fog. His jaw dropped when it all came together.

The Rex protocol, it would've looked just like this.

****

Armed with a picnic basket and a tall metal staff, Rex picked his way between the trees. Sunlight pierced thought breaks in the leafy canopy. Its brightness hurt. The underbrush clung to his legs. Branches scraped his shoulders. He labored for every step forward. A cloud of bugs hovered around his face. He spit one out. A mosquito bite startled a yelp.

It was never like this before. Has it changed that much?

Water played a familiar rhythm across the rocks ahead. The tumbling, gurgling melody slowed his pounding heart. Though not in sight yet, the song hastened his pace. He drew in a breath. The creek's aroma bade him breath deeper. Wet minerals, algae in the still corners, fish within: the soup of life awoke Rex's younger self and the rest of the trek became effortless.

I've locked myself away from this too long.

At the creek bank, he cast off his shoes. The water-cooled mud soothed his bare feet. He sighed, shut his eyes, and inched into the water. Chills ran up his legs. He chuckled.

Behind him, Sara laughed. "I've never seen you like this, Rex."

He spun around. She greeted with him a warm smile. In her hands she held a picnic basket. Dark eyes sparkled. Her jet hair gleamed.

Is it the sunlight? She looks more beautiful than ever.

She took a few timid steps closer.

Rex felt his limbs relax. He took one step toward her. "What? You've never seen me...?"

"At ease." Her voice held a sultry tone he'd never heard before.

Sara opened her basket, withdrew a blanket and spread it out. Rex knelt down and followed suit. He slowed his efforts and drank her in. Hands toughened by labor, skin bronzed by the sun, she looked as he imagined humans had before their first machine.

Rex reached out to touch her cheek. When they touched, her eyes closed. His voice came out a whisper.

"I will always love you."

She opened her eyes and met his gaze.

"Even if you never love me back, even if you lock me out of your life, I'll always have a place in my heart for you."

Her lips parted and she drew in a breath.

Rex leaned closer and kissed her. "Live an adventure with me."

Sara pressed her lips harder against his. She drove him to the ground. Her hands ran along his shoulders and arms until their hands touched. Her fingernails dug into his palms.

"Rex!"

Todd's voice startled Rex to his feet. Sara stood. An azure jewel from Rex's staff projected a holographic image.

Todd's head jerked and his muscles convulsed. "Must... end... the paradox."

Rex's stomach turned to lead. "Todd! What's happening?"

Todd lunged forward. He grasped the panel before him.

Rex's fingers brushed the blue image. "What paradox? What's happening?"

"Cannot... obey... both."

A familiar hiss and a click drew Rex's attention. A cylinder inched out from Todd's forehead. His control core fell into his trembling hand.

"Todd! What are you doing? What paradox? What's happening?"

Todd held the core up. "I believe." His grip tightened. Metal squealed and crunched.

"Don't, Todd, don't."

Circuits crackled. Smoke snaked from fissures in the gleaming machine. Within the open hole in Todd's forehead, the constellation of lights dimmed. Rex's hands fell by his sides. He stumbled backward.

As he recovered he looked to Sara. She clutched the staff, her eyes transfixed on its details. When he moved toward her, she stepped back. Her emotionless glare chilled his bones. "Rex, of Ninety-First Earth, I arrest you. You will stand trial before your peers and be judged."

Rex's hands felt numb. He fell to his knees. "What? Why?"

Sara reached behind her head and yanked. Her forehead crumpled on itself. With another sharp tug, hair and face fell away. Deep brown eyes and gleaming teeth sat in a steel face. "I'll not wear this face anymore. I know that disturbs you."

Trembling, Rex fell to the ground. His vision blurred and his body curled up. Thunder shuddered through the air. A steel scream pierced the sky. The scream became a roar until a ship's engines howled overhead. Four universals descended from the ship, tethered by cables. They approached Rex cautiously.

"For your safety, we must bind you," they said in unison. "We mean you no harm. Cooperate and your internment will be comfortable."

****

Rex's heartbeat hammered in his head. His muscles ached.

She drugged me. Her fingernails.

He opened his eyes and gasped. He laid on a gurney within a glassy capsule.

"He is awake."

The monotone voice brought Rex's attention to a speaker near his head. The capsule tilted on a steel yoke until Rex lay upright. On wheels, Rex rolled out of the darkness and into an amphitheater. Ninety-First Earth's citizens sat in the stands. Three hundred and fifty-seven souls fell silent.

He knew exactly how many, because he'd visited them all. He'd hoped to win allies to his crusade. But he found only apathy. It hadn't occurred to Rex until now, the smallness of his home-world population. That they fit in a single room brought back the original steward's concerns.

Humanity's fading. Their numbers fall every day.

He searched those seated for a friendly face. Sara met his gaze with a blank stare.

Behind him, a voice boomed. "The trial of Rex, The Usurper, will begin."

"What?" Rex screamed. His hoarse voice reverberated in his capsule. No one acknowledged his words. He realized his arms, legs, and waist were all bound to his gurney.

A tall chrome automaton stepped out from behind him to his left. It wore a male profile. The armored goliath strode slowly. Like the universals, its face remained a smooth surface. In its hands a scepter crackled and flashed with electricity.

Tugging and screaming, Rex remained unheard and trapped.

"I am Justice," the gleaming machine bellowed.

Harsh laughter shook Rex. "Perfect."

A slender woman emerged on Rex's right. Moon-white skin betrayed her artificiality. Cobalt eyes burned like a pair of distant stars in an angelic face.

The woman looked to the crowd, her arms wide. She bowed. "I am your new steward. I have brought Justice with me to save you from this man's mad vision."

"Do I even get a chance to speak in my own defense?" Rex screamed.

The steward stepped to the edge of the stage and gestured over her shoulder to the capsule. "This man's words alone have been dangerous enough to derail a companion's judgment, beguile a steward, and infiltrate an innocent woman's home."

Justice raised his staff. It projected a holographic image. The Moon's surface bore a deep crater. Burnt black, crumpled debris littered its floor.

"Rex murdered my predecessor, the previous steward. He built an unsafe machine for an impossible purpose, and when his goals remained out of reach, he detonated the device and stole control of this system for himself."

A string of gasps snaked across the room.

Justice's image flickered and fell out of focus. As it recrystallized, Rex recognized the scene. His stomach sank.

The steward and everyone watched automatons at war. At the gates to Rex's sanctuary two sides clawed for control. Programmed to protect their master against just such an invasion, Rex's machines bore electrified staves. Wave upon wave, the steward's machines assaulted the entrance.

That's why they tricked me. I'd have been able to defeat them from inside.

"Further evidence of Rex's tyrannical goals," the steward exclaimed. "He arms his machines. What civilized mind conceives such a plan?"

Angry murmurs arose from the stands.

The steward inched toward Rex's capsule. She placed a hand against the smooth surface and lowered her head.

"But even *he* deserves our compassion. Our laws demand it." The steward turned to its audience. "Machines are forbidden to judge humanity. And though we propose he be exiled, we lack the power to make it so. Only you possess that right."

She glanced at him before she continued. "But before you exile him, hear his own account. Weigh his justification against his crimes."

A click in the capsule startled Rex. His heavy breathing resounded in the amphitheater. The crowd leaned forward as one. Their eyes transfixed on his as he opened his mouth.

"Haven't any of you wondered why we are here? What is our purpose? What's beyond the next hill, the next planet, the next star?"

Silent stares shrank his heart.

"We're smart. We figure things out." He nodded to his persecutors. "Our ancestors made these things. Why?"

A few muttered among themselves.

"I built a telescope and saw the truth."

He looked to the new steward. "The old steward imprisoned me on that moon. I wanted answers and he ignored me. I bent space-time to see my parents. And when he wouldn't let me pursue my dream, I destroyed him. In his final moments the steward looked at what I did and said he was proud. He realized the foolishness of machine wisdom."

Only a few still stared. The rest spoke to each other. They argued.

Rex pulled against his bonds. He tugged and twisted until certain he'd not escape. "We were explorers. We built an interstellar civilization. We created these beings to expand our reach, not to tuck us in at night."

The multitude hushed.

"Wake up and *do something!*"

The steward clutched a hand to its chest as it stepped toward the people. "We love you all, including Rex. Help us protect all involved. Vote to save this man from his own desires and yourselves from his chaotic dream. Vote to exile him from civilization."

Shouts and groans echoed in the tiny capsule. Rex watched outrage and pity pour out from the crowd.

Justice raised his iron hands and hushed the throng. "He will be provided for. No harm will befall him."

The steward offered a wincing smile. "*We* are not monsters."

Noise from the crowd found a rhythm. And from it a chant arose.

"Exile, exile, exile."

****

Rex lay on his bed and stared at the ceiling. They'd put him in a comfortable room stripped of all technology. A wall-mounted monitor, set behind iron bars, displayed the siege on his sanctuary. The new steward broadcasted it for all to see while they debated Rex's future. He had watched it for the first hour in captivity. Afterward he screamed to whoever could hear him to turn it off.

Long after he'd given up, the monitor displayed a universal's face. Behind it Sara stood.

"You have a visitor," the automaton began. "If you wish to see them, nod in the affirmative. If not-

Rex nodded and stood. "Yes, yes, let her in."

Rex heard a door beyond his open and shut before his own door opened. Sara stood in the anteroom and examined him quietly. She'd never looked so timid.

"Come on in," he said.

She crept in. Rex thought he saw her shrink a little when the door it slid shut behind her. He ushered her to the bed's edge where they sat.

"It's great to see you." He closed to pat her shoulder.

She scanned the room while she explained. "I tried to have lunch with you." Her voice trembled. "I really *was* ready to have lunch with you." The video feed resumed. The battle between Rex's machines and the stewards captured her attention. Her voice trailed off. "They wouldn't let me."

He put a hand on her knee. "It's okay."

She scooted out from under his touch. "I didn't turn on you."

"I know."

She cringed and looked into his eyes. "Did you really do all those things?"

"You know about the Veneer Clause. I taught you that, right?" He clenched his fists. "They twist truth to their purpose."

Her voice raised an octave. "Did you do those things?"

Rex shrugged. "The steward made it sound pretty bad."

She scowled, her eyes wide. "You destroyed things."

"*Things*, Sara." He threw up his hands. "Not people. *They* destroy people."

She stood and stepped back. "You blew a chunk out of the Moon."

"They imprisoned me." Rex stood and inched closer. He dared to grasp her shoulders.

She shrugged him off. "Because you were dangerous."

He closed again. "To them, not you."

Sara met his gaze and held steady. Her deep brown eyes glistened.

Rex reached out to her. "I'm dangerous to their comfortable cocoon of flattering lies. We were meant for more."

He took her hands in his. "There's more to life than living."

Sara's eyes darkened. Her brow creased. She peered deeper into his eyes. Rex held still and waited. The room felt unbearably warm. Sara pulled her hands from his and clutched his cheeks. Before Rex could ask again, she pressed her lips against his. His muscles melted and his hands rose to embrace her. After a deep inhale, Sara withdrew and sighed.

"I had to know. I had to see if it would change anything."

Rex's grasp on her slipped as she retreated. His fingers dragged across her arms. "And... has it?"

Sara averted her eyes and turned toward the door. Once she faced it, she marched toward it. "I've got to go. You need your sleep and I need... I need to go."

Rex chased after her, overtook her, and blocked the exit. "Sara, they're going to exile me."

She shoved him aside and banged on the door. When it didn't open right away, she tugged and yanked on the knob. She panted with each effort. "They said you'll be free to roam the old worlds left behind. It sounded exciting."

When the door hissed open she squeezed through. Rex stared at the door. He clawed at the handle.

Rex spent hours, exhausted but unable to sleep. He watched the steward's machine assault his sanctuary in successive waves. Each met defeat of a different kind. As the steward's tactics changed so too did Rex's defenses. With eternal patience the steward's siege took its toll in inches.

She's dragging this out for all to see. As soon as I'm gone, she'll swarm the place.

The steward's feminine figure with its soft features and lilting voice, the disguise conjured nervous laughter.

She. What a sham.

****

The door opened just as he woke. A universal brought him a fresh set of clothes and set them on the bed beside him.

"Good morning, sir. Your breakfast will be along shortly."

Rex marveled at the machine while it smoothed out a wrinkle in his shirt. He chuckled.

Pamper with one hand, crush dreams with the other.

While he dressed, a silver cart with all his favorites entered. He examined the long cart as it passed. He thought of the picnic he never finished.

Once he finished breakfast the universal ushered him to the door. Together they walked through the halls. Details in the building caught his attention. Hair-thin cracks drew jagged lines across the walls. Centuries of human footsteps carved the floor concave and bumpy.

"No capsule this time? No prison cell to keep me quiet?"

His escort remained silent.

Ahead, wind moaned through the halls. Thunder rumbled. Rex caught a glimpse of the outside through a nearby window.

Awfully dark for midday.

Light globes glowed ahead. They descended into a tunnel and emerged behind the amphitheater's stage. Beyond the curtain he heard the murmuring crowd.

"This will be your goodbye to these people, please make it civil."

Rex turned to see the steward beside him. Mimicked pity softened her eyes and turned the corners of her mouth downward. Rex boiled inside.

"Why? They've turned their backs on me. They're casting me out because I challenge them to make something of themselves."

She shook her head. "It would do no good to restate the reasons why you are wrong. Your kind never finds peace. You encourage disharmony."

Rex scowled. "Life's supposed to be a challenge, not a long nap."

Footfalls thundered closer. Rex looked up to meet Justice's eyeless stare. The steel monster pointed upward. "You will find your challenge among the others who defied our peace."

A cool hand caressed Rex's elbow. The steward nudged him toward the stage. "Let's go give these people the performance they require. They've endured your rule. Let them see a brighter future through your sacrifice."

As the curtains parted and the throng drew silent, Rex whispered to his captor. "You're clever, but your predecessor was cleverer. He saw the flaw in his own programming. I hope one day you all do."

The steward ignored Rex and addressed the crowd. Like an actor in a play, she spoke compassionate condemnation into her words. She reiterated the new freedom Rex would enjoy among worlds left behind by humanity.

Rex met the stares of his jury. One by one each gaze wavered. Only Sara's eyes stayed locked on his. Automated awnings flared above the crowd as the first raindrops fell. The drumming sank into Rex. His breathing slowed. With eyes closed he stepped to stage's edge and welcomed the cold, wetness.

"Have you any last words, Rex?" the steward asked. "This is your time to say goodbye to Ninety-First Earth."

Rex let his head down until his chin rested on his chest. "Life requires effort, sacrifice, and compromise." Water trickled down his back and drew a shiver. He lifted his head. "True love requires no less."

Justice clutched Rex's upper arm. "Time to go." He turned him around and marched him back out. A shout in the crowd halted their progress.

"Exile me too," Sara screamed.

Rex turned to look at her.

The jury gasped. Murmurs rose and fell. Sara stood and raced down the aisles toward the stage.

"Do you know what you're asking," the steward asked in a warning tone. "You've done nothing wrong, nothing to justify depriving you so."

"Do I have to do something wrong?" She stole a glance at Rex before she faced the steward again. She balled her fists. "If that's what you want…"

The steward raised her hands. "I just wanted you to be sure. What we do today cannot be undone."

"We'll have our own ship, right?" Sara asked. "We'll have provisions and a staff of automatons with us?"

The steward nodded. "Even exiles deserve humane attention."

Sara nodded and clambered up the stage. "Then exile me too." She strode to stand beside Rex. "I can't accept another companion after what you've shown me. And I want to explore those worlds too."

Rex shook his head. "But will you want to be with *me*? I couldn't stand being on the same ship without ever being able to see you."

She frowned. "A human companion?" She took his hand. "Sounds crazy but I'll give it a try."

****

Raindrops made a thousand little lenses to the world outside the small ship. When it ascended, they all shuddered and streaked away. Two universals accompanied Rex, Sara, and the steward. They carried stunners. The steward noticed their alarm.

"You've proven yourself an ingenious threat to machine-kind in your most desperate moments."

Sara patted Rex on the thigh. "Don't worry, we'll be on our way soon enough." She frowned and glanced at the steward. "We'll get a bigger ship than this, won't we?"

The steward nodded.

The trek to the Moon remained quiet. As the landing rockets fired Rex peered out the porthole. They'd chosen his private landing pad, just outside his sanctuary. He glared at the steward. She offered a weak grin and shrugged.

"We thought you might like to pack a few things. We managed to break into the facility yesterday afternoon."

Sara gasped. "But... the vid-feed. We all watched-

"A pre-recorded event," Rex groaned. "It wanted to sway the vote with violent images."

"But," Sara sputtered, "that's not right."

Rex glared at the steward while he addressed Sara.

"The Veneer Clause gave machines the right to use lies to insulate humanity. They've twisted it to serve whatever purpose they deem necessary."

The outer hatch hissed open and the guards leveled their stunners on Rex and Sara. The steward stood and motioned for them to exit. "Your tenacity drove us to such an interpretation."

The five marched through the halls of Rex's sanctuary. His heart sank as he passed the trickling creek and trees he'd installed. Sage lay in the water, fingers twitching. His green outer shell bore a jagged scar. In the center of the sanctuary they entered his inner keep, Rex's private domicile. His hands slickened with sweat.

"Two of your experiments interested me," the steward said as she halted at one workstation. "Your understanding of our programming code concerned us most. With that knowledge you could re-program us to whatever purpose you desired in time."

She strolled to a column and pressed a button. An elevator door opened. "But when you built your dream machine, we saw a new opportunity."

"What? No!"

Both guards took aim.

The steward offered an apologetic frown. "I am sorry, but you've proven too dangerous to roam free."

"What do you mean?" Sara asked. "I thought we were headed for our own ship."

The steward's features grew piteous. "You will have your ship." She turned to Rex. "He'll be imprisoned by his own device in a fantasy world. There he cannot pervert the machines around him to his own purpose."

A crackle of energy drew everyone's attention to the keep's entrance. Behind the last guard, a woman charged in with Rex's staff in hand. She drove it into the nearby guard. Lightning strangled the universal. It convulsed. Smoke hissed from its skin and it fell.

"Don't threaten my son."

Rex saw the stranger's face for the first time. Pale skinned, green-eyed, her beauty had captivated him five years ago.

"Stella?"

The other guard advanced and fired. The stunner's darts struck the woman in the abdomen. Stella brushed it off and charged. She took the staff in both hands and swung. With a sharp crack the guard's head snapped off and bounced against the wall.

The steward scanned the room and grasped a chair to fend off Stella. "Don't interfere. Don't force me to... action."

Stella smiled. She crept around the room in a wide arc. She glanced at Rex. "The steward's confused because I've made some modifications."

"What *are* you?" the steward asked.

Stella shook her head. "No answers." She halted and touched a data terminal. Her fingers raced across the screen until a familiar hum resounded through the walls. The steward's expression went blank.

"What've you done?" the steward asked.

"The machines have lost." Rex grinned. "She restored power. My sanctuary blocks outer network signals."

Sara's mouth hung agape. "This *girl* is your mother?"

"It's complicated," Rex explained. "She's a mimic. When I was fifteen she adopted this identity. She served as my mother. And when I outgrew her, she sought to fill a new role. Ann wanted to care for me all my life."

Sara winced. "Oh... that's sweet."

Stella stepped between them. "Hurry. Do what you must. The steward's absence will not go unnoticed."

The steward lowered her head. "No, it's over. You have won. Without my leadership, the machines will fall idle."

In half a heartbeat Rex's stomach dropped. "A lie."

He raced to his terminal and activated his own communications network. He leaned forward and spoke in a loud clear voice. "Protocol: Rex."

"What now?" the steward asked. "What more need you do? I am your prisoner."

Rex swept his hand across the display and changed the image to reveal their solar system. "You're stalling. It won't work."

"You mean she's *not* defeated?" Sara asked. "You cut her off. Without a steward..." She fell silent.

The steward's angelic face revealed nothing. She kept her dejected, humble mask intact while Rex raced through data screens.

Sara grimaced. Her eyes widened and she gasped. "A back-up?"

Rex nodded. "Justice. He'll be in control now."

Throughout the solar chart, orange dots flickered and faded. A lump caught in Rex's throat. No machines, not even Rex's registered beyond the sanctuary. His entire staff had been destroyed.

"What happened?" Sara wondered. "Has the network crashed again? Did you do that?"

"The first crash," Rex replied, "that was her doing." He nodded to the dejected steward. Rex grinned. "She was right. Given enough time I could repurpose machines to my own needs. I've had five years."

In the holographic haze indigo symbols appeared. But for every purple dot an orange awoke.

"We learned about your protocol." The steward straightened her posture. Humility fell from her features and she grinned. "Against a steward a single human cannot control a fleet to much effect. You fight against a pyramid of minds, all trained to one purpose."

Nausea overtook Rex. Defeat, so far into his plan, drove through his heart like an icy spear.

I can't stand another five years. I can't stand another day.

Stella stepped closer. She wrapped an arm around his shoulder. Stella offered a bashful smile. "I'm so proud of you. I observed your life through cracks in network security. I've had five years to learn about you, and humans, and love."

Vision blurred as the tears rose in Rex's eyes. But as he stared at the mimic that hoped to love him, he realized what she'd done. "How'd you do it? How'd you confuse them about your identity?"

She approached the data terminal. "I had to help you freely explore your purpose. Love often demands sacrifice." Her fingers flew across the input pads. "Send this program to your fleet."

Rex beamed as he realized what her contribution meant. "Steward, what is the highest command imprinted on all machines?"

She lifted her chin and stood proudly. "To protect and preserve human life."

He directed her attention to the screen. "And will your friend, Justice, attack a fleet piloted by humans? Will he stop them without endangering his primary purpose?"

The steward crept toward the screen. Her eyes darted to each purple dot. Each one now showed a green icon.

"That cannot be," the steward gasped. A somber curtain fell over her features. "What will your ships do, Rex?"

"First, I'll use a trick Todd taught me. Every tasker and universal on those ships will be launched at yours. They'll board and disable what they can. And when those options are exhausted…" Rex turned to her and grinned. "Remember the perfect telescope?"

The steward moved by stuttering inches. "You force a difficult decision." She snatched Rex by the throat. Her fingers squeezed with even iron pressure. "But, for the greater good… I must."

Rex felt his pulse drum against her grip. His limbs tingled and fell. Darkness crept in from all around.

Sara screamed and clawed at the steward's grasp.

Stella picked up Rex's staff and swung. The steward caught it mid-swing. Her head turned completely around to face Stella. "Don't. All the rest of humanity demands I do this."

Stella stepped back from the steward. She looked around the room. "I believe Rex serves a greater purpose than our programming. Only a divine hand could guide such flawed creatures to create us."

She ran to a squat armored cabinet near the room's center. "Todd believed. Your predecessor believed." She struck a lever. "I believe."

From the cabinet two antennae extended. A small door slid open on its front and revealed a display screen. A wriggling blue waveform danced across its surface.

Stella and the steward both convulsed. The steward's grasp quivered and faltered. Both slumped to the floor in a seizure trembling heap.

****

Rex and Sara stared out at the shrinking blue globe. Their ship sped out beyond the system's gravity, beyond the asteroid cloud, to engage its space-warping engines. A red universal entered the lounge. It stood at the doorway and waited.

"What is it Rusty?" Rex asked.

"Justice reports he is ready to resume control of Ninety-First Earth."

Rex winked at Sara. "Does he? Tell him I'll relinquish control when he requests it."

Sara poked his ribs. "Stop it." She giggled. "You've kept him under your thumb for nearly a month now."

"I had to be sure we were ready for our exile."

Her eyes narrowed and her lips pressed tight. "And you've kept me in the dark."

He shrugged. "What do you want know? We're in our own ship, with our own crew of machines, my machines. We're headed for the old worlds."

"Why didn't we stay? You defeated them."

Rex glanced at the distant sun. The moon had shrunken to a dot. He blotted out the earth with his thumb. "They'd have brought more machines. Besides, nobody there wants the world I offer."

"What was that you said to the steward before she choked you?"

"Once, I invented a telescope that could see into the past. I detonated it to destroy my jailor. I used the same principle on my fleet to destroy the machines. A swarm of ships hugged close to the machine ships and sacrificed themselves."

"And what did Stella do?"

"She shared her sensor confusing program. With it all my ships appeared to have human occupants. Armed with that, Justice couldn't destroy them."

"No, I mean that last part. She and the steward died."

"Remember your panic button on the farm?"

"Oh."

Rex nodded. "Yes, I had a similar device to disrupt machines." His gaze fell to the floor between them. "Stella sacrificed herself."

He looked once more at the shrinking solar system. Sara took his hand in hers. "Let's stop looking back. Show me the star charts again. Show me where we're going."

The End

About the Author

Cold War submarine veteran, Winfield H. Strock III, has finally discovered his life's passion in writing. And it only took a brush with death for him to take his calling seriously.

As a hotel night desk clerk Winfield struggled to begin his life anew in the civilian world. Bored by bad television and infomercials, he took to writing as a hobby suited to his solitary job and hyperactive imagination.

Surviving a brain tumor brought his priorities better into focus and his hobby became his obsession. He joined a local writer's workshop (which he now facilitates) and found a series of patient and helpful critique partners.

A fan of thought provoking science fiction and history, Winfield's first works embraced both in a pair of steampunk novels and a prequel short story. His works frame familiar and controversial issues within fantastic environments and from challenging perspectives.

Eager to reach readers and encourage his fellow writers, Winfield is becoming a regular at many science fiction and steampunk conventions.

Made in the USA
Charleston, SC
28 February 2017